Josie

A STORY OF FORGIVENESS

Karen G. Bruce

Jan-Carol
Publishing, Inc
"every story needs a book"

Josie: A Story of Forgiveness
Written by Karen G. Bruce

Published October 2021
Little Creek Books
Imprint of Jan-Carol Publishing, Inc.
All rights reserved
Copyright © 2021 Karen G. Bruce

ISBN: 978-1-954978-28-7
Library of Congress Control Number: 2021949057

You may contact the publisher:
Jan-Carol Publishing, Inc.
PO Box 701
Johnson City, TN 37605
publisher@jancarolpublishing.com
www.jancarolpublishing.com

I would like to dedicate this book to my husband, Kenny Bruce.
Thank you for being you. I love you more than I can ever say in words.

Author's Note

This story is completely fictional but I think it's a story that people can relate to in some manner, whether it involves a spouse that has cheated, a parent who is facing a devastating illness, or family secrets that can turn your whole world upside down. Forgiveness is not always easy; it's oftentimes something that is easier said than done. Can you forgive? Can you forget? Everyone's story is different, but holding on to your hurt can choose your path in life, whether it's moving on or holding back. As the title says, it's Josie's story of forgiveness and what she ultimately chooses for her life.

PART I:

Past and Present

Chapter 1

I had come to a point in my life that if I didn't make some changes soon, I was going to go, as old Mr. Gibbons used to say, "Crazier than a shithouse rat." Mr. Gibbons worked on my daddy's farm during the summers, and Mama usually wouldn't let me get near him because of his colorful language. When I was little, I wasn't sure what crazy meant, but I knew it had to be pretty bad. I made the mistake of telling my teacher in the first grade that Tommy Altizer was crazier than a shithouse rat when he chased me all over the playground and tried to kiss me on the lips. We both ended up in the principal's office.

For months my life had consisted of putting one foot in front of the other. After losing my mother to cancer, just getting through each day without falling apart was all I could hope to accomplish. Sadness and weariness would sometimes overwhelm me to the point of indescribable pain. To cope meant I had to become numb, but the numbness in my body was beginning to revive and wake up. The fog was lifting and my extremities were tingling; the problem was I didn't like seeing the person I had become. I was invisible in a way, to myself and to others, fading into nothing.

Somehow, through that fading fog I decided I didn't want to be nothing. I wanted to live. I wanted to laugh again, or at least smile every once in a while. Life wasn't worth living if you didn't live (I'm sure I heard this little tidbit somewhere). You might as well be dead. Being

1

numb wasn't living. How had I functioned every day? My recollection of the last year was very unclear, and that was a scary feeling.

Emerging from the numbness and fog, feelings I had held at bay for so long were beginning to surface. They were conflicting, these feelings. If I smiled or laughed, would it mean that my mother hadn't been important to me? Would living a full, content life be a betrayal to her? She had been one of the most important people in my life, so how could I live my life without her and be happy? I missed her. I missed calling her every day whenever I had a question or thought, or just for any reason. I missed having that special someone who knew me inside and out and loved me anyway, flaws and all. She loved me, period. Would anyone else ever love me like that? A mother's love is fierce, protective, and never fails. At least, my mother's love was.

Deep down, I knew that life must go on, that holding myself back wasn't normal. There were other important people in my life: my husband and children, to name a few. I knew it wasn't fair to them. I couldn't remember the last real conversation I'd had with my husband. We didn't talk anymore, unless we had to. What was the last thing I said? "Pass the salt? Don't forget to take out the garbage? Fix that annoying leaky faucet?" My boys deserved a mama who was present and accounted for, even if they were at an age that they didn't need me quite so much. I needed to be there; I *wanted* to be there.

It wasn't fair to my father and sister either, even though sometimes I thought they could care less anyway. My mother was the glue that held our family together. My father suffered from Alzheimer's, and my sister did most of the caregiving. My sister, Mary, was stubborn; she felt it was her responsibility alone to take care of our father, for some reason. She would only ask me to help when she absolutely had to, and I was guilty of letting her. It was easier that way. Without my mother, we were all drifting apart.

My job as a postal worker included delivering mail. I didn't communicate much with anyone, except for Mrs. Jenkins. She was on my mail route. She always seemed to know what to say, and didn't expect much from me. She could talk to a wall and the conversation would still be lively. Sometimes I was the wall.

The day my mom found out she had cancer changed my life. She fought hard, but in the end the cancer won. Losing her was like losing a part of myself. Mary was always jealous of our relationship; she said I was Mom's favorite, which secretly I thought was true. We did have a special bond. I was more like her, and Mary was more like our dad. We were romantics, and they were pragmatics. We were loving and affectionate, and they...well, they were not.

It was time for a change. I had this realization on a Sunday morning in late spring, as I was getting ready for church. I was going to the same church I had attended my whole life in our small town in Southwest Virginia. The morning began like any other. I got up and made the coffee, and John went out to feed the chickens, pigs, and cows. We hardly spoke as we ate our eggs and toast, or in the truck on the way to church. As we headed for our usual pew, I suddenly stopped. Looking at John, I said, "Let's sit somewhere else."

John looked at me as if I was speaking in tongues, which would have been highly inappropriate in our small-town Baptist church. I could just picture everyone staring, looking at me like I was deranged. The only speaking in tongues around happened in the old-fashioned churches, in the mountains or hollows. Old Dr. Reed's office would be full of whiplash patients come Monday morning from all the head turning.

"I'm serious." Getting excited, I pointed to an empty space. "We can sit there."

After a puzzled moment, John, shrugged his shoulders and said, "Fine." I smiled for the first time that day, glad that I at least did *something* different. It wasn't much, but it broke the monotony. It felt good. Maybe this was all I needed. A change in routine could do wonders. Unfortunately, some people didn't like this particular change.

Just as I was beginning to feel some satisfaction, I heard someone say, "What are you doing sitting in our seats, Josie?" I turned to find Ed Johnson staring at me as if we had committed some horrible offense. I noticed, of course, that only my name was mentioned. Why did he assume it was me instead of John?

Ed, Linda, and their teenage daughter were waiting for us to exit the pew so that they could sit down in what they assumed were their assigned church seats. Ed was wearing his maroon suit, the same one he wore every other Sunday. When he was feeling particularly spunky, he would wear his fish tie with it. Fish ties are not attractive, especially his fish tie; it had a small, possibly permanent grease stain on the large-mouth bass in the center of the tie where his food apparently dropped on a regular basis. I guess he thought we wouldn't notice the stain. He was wrong.

John started to get up but I pulled his arm abruptly, causing him to sigh and settle back down. Something inside me snapped. "I don't see your name on this pew, Ed. Why can't y'all sit somewhere else?" By the look on his face, I could see I was fighting a losing battle. I'd known Ed for a long time, and he had about as much imagination as a doorknob. Their daughter Victoria looked annoyed, but then again, she always looked annoyed. I'm sure she couldn't wait to Tweet about it. Linda looked at her husband as if she was confused. *Poor thing*, I thought. *If she's depending on Ed Johnson for guidance, then she's in a sorry mess.*

We were attracting some attention from people already seated. Mrs. Riddle, one of our deacons' wives, who happened to be sitting in the row in front of us, was eavesdropping as usual. In her slightly nasal voice, she said, "Josie, what in the world has gotten into you? You know the Johnsons have been sittin' in that pew for years." Poor, boring Mrs. Riddle. If she ever did something close to wild and crazy in her life, it was probably the time she wore white after Labor Day. I remember the day well. Mrs. Tulley, another one of our esteemed deacons' wives, actually called her out on it. "You do know it's after Labor Day, don't you, Betty?" Mrs. Riddle had sputtered a string of excuses, muttering "It's ninety degrees outside, for goodness' sakes," and walked out of the vestibule in a huff. Most of our deacons' wives were as sweet as could be, but there were a couple (Mrs. Riddle and Mrs. Tulley) who thought they were a little more special than the rest.

Mrs. Tulley was in charge of our shut-in program, making sure all those members who couldn't come to church because of sickness or other ailments were prayed for and had the occasional meal or care package. Southern Baptists love to eat. Mrs. Tulley also had a big head (in more ways than one) and felt it was her duty to give her opinion in all matters, whether it was wanted or not. Mrs. Riddle happened to be one of those who did not appreciate it, although she still liked to give her own opinions quite frequently.

Feeling frustrated and ill with the world, I stood up with determination and looked around. There were plenty of seats available, so I pointed to an area a couple of rows up. "Look! Those seats are empty. You know, people...y'all don't have to sit in the same seats every Sunday. It's not a rule! Change is good! Why can't y'all be different for once in your lives?" The more I talked, the louder my voice rose. I knew it was getting bad because I tended to say y'all a lot when I got excited. Eventually, I had the whole congregation staring at me as if I had lost my marbles. John's head was down and his fingers were rubbing the area between his eyes. Suddenly, I realized it was pointless; these people just didn't get it. I was only making myself look crazy, or at least like I had lost my will to hide it. Old Mr. Gibbons would be proud, and would most certainly call me out on it. It's funny how I always thought of that old man.

With as much dignity as I could muster, I stood up and walked out of the church. Feeling everyone's eyes following me made me want to run, but I held myself in check and took measured steps, head held high until I reached the parking lot, hoping they wouldn't see that maybe I was crazier than a shithouse rat.

I stopped by John's truck and sat down on the curb, wishing I had a cigarette. I had quit a few years before but every once in a while, the cravings would hit me like a cast iron skillet, right upside the head. At that moment, I would have paid a hundred bucks for just one cigarette. I could just imagine tearing the cellophane wrapper off of the box, smelling the sweet tobacco, taking that first, wonderful drag, and feeling the buzz go straight to my head. Why *did* I quit, anyway? All the reasons were valid and important at the time, but none seemed very significant at that moment.

Eventually John walked over to where I sat and leaned against the truck, his shadow blocking the late morning sun. For a moment, he just stood there, saying nothing. He had his hands in his trouser pockets and as usual, looked very uncomfortable in his Sunday suit. John was a big man: six feet tall, towering over my five-foot-two frame. He held his hand out for me to take. In silent resignation I let him pull me slowly to my feet. We got in the truck and headed back to the farm. John was not one for small talk, or for showing too much emotion in public. At home he was more affectionate—or he used to be, anyway.

Now that the fog was lifting, clarity began setting in. We were definitely growing apart. His quiet strength had always made me feel safe and loved, but lately it felt different. As John pulled into the driveway, I was determined to do what I needed to do to make things better between us. I knew that the distance between us was probably my fault. We silently got out of the truck, walking towards the cabin we built 15 years ago on my parents' farm. I remember the day we moved in. The smell of wood in our cabin was like an intoxicating fragrance to me. It was so fresh and clean, not like the old farmhouse I grew up in that had years of strange, odd smells; no matter how much you cleaned, it still smelled old. The windows in the cabin were snug and tight, the wrap-around porch was heavenly, and the new appliances were a dream. The boys loved the two-bedroom loft upstairs that they had all to themselves. We had worked extremely hard towards the dream of building our very own log cabin, so when we finally moved in, it was that much sweeter.

Ricky and Lucy, our farm dogs, greeted us as if we had been away for weeks instead of the 30 minutes it took for me to cause a scene at church and leave. Even though someone had thoughtlessly discarded the brother and sister at the pound, we were lucky enough to find them, bring them home, and turn them loose. They were a collie-shepherd mix and had the sweetest temperaments, but were also protective. We never had to worry about wild animals on our property. Ricky was pretty laid back but Lucy felt it was her duty to protect us, and she did it with a vengeance.

They looked almost identical, except for a dark patch on Lucy's nose. After giving them both a head rub, I walked up the front porch steps and sat down in one of our wooden rockers. Sensing my unhappiness, Lucy curled up at my feet, then slowly rolled over on her back. Smiling, I rubbed her belly with my foot.

John followed me and sat down. We rocked in silence except for the occasional farm animal sounds. Between the cows and the chickens, it was hardly ever quiet at the farm, but it was a comforting noise. An occasional gaggle of geese would fly down the path of the river honking away, announcing their arrival and subsequent departure as well.

I looked at John, who was staring out at nothing in particular. "What's wrong with me, John?"

"You're just having a bad day, Josie." I shook my head because I knew it was more than just a bad day. I had realized I was losing part of myself, and it scared me. I couldn't be content anymore with the humdrum life. I was so tired of it, and I definitely needed more. Was John satisfied with the way things had become?

It wasn't that long ago that we couldn't get enough of each other. Now I wouldn't cause a stir if I walked through the house naked. I used to do that just for fun and John would say, "Lord help us, Josie's got her groove on." Now he would probably say, "Can you hand me the remote?"

The silence between us was beginning to suffocate me. In frustration, I turned to him and said, "I think it's a little more than a 'bad day,' John. This..." I pointed at him and then at myself. "This isn't normal." I shook my head. "There's something wrong here, and I don't like it."

John shrugged. His silence was telling, and it scared me to death.

"I don't know about you, but I can't stand it. Things need to change between us. I know I haven't been easy to live with lately, and I'm sorry." I was surprised that I actually voiced my feelings and that we were talking... or at least I was.

"John." I looked at him and then looked down, ashamed of what I had become. "John, I'm sorry for the way I've acted since Mama died." When he didn't say anything, I looked up and studied his face. He sat there, silent, with a blank look that I couldn't read.

"John? Can you talk to me, please?"

John got up and leaned against the porch rail, facing me. "What do you want me to say, Josie?" The look on his face frightened me. Was it too late?

In frustration I scooted to the edge of the rocking chair. "I want you to tell me everything is going to be okay. I want you say you still love me."

John crossed his arms. He looked like he was trying to speak but couldn't find the words.

I stood up and yelled, "*Really?!* That's all ya got? Our marriage has turned into a stinky pile of manure, and you don't know what to say?!"

Before I began crying and making a fool of myself, I ran into the house and headed for our bedroom. After I shut the door, I sat down on the bed and thought about when my life was just beginning, when I had so much hope. Was it that long ago?

Chapter 2

I'll never forget the first time I laid eyes on John. It was the beginning of my ninth-grade year of high school, and he was a year older. I was late for class and barely had time to get to my locker, grab my book for the next class, and run down the hallway. In my rush I accidentally bumped into him, causing us both to drop our books. Taking my arm, John looked at me and said, "Whoa! What's your hurry?"

I guess I must have been standing there with my mouth hanging wide open because John grinned, causing my face to turn ten shades of red. He had the most gorgeous green eyes I had ever seen, ringed with long, dark eyelashes. His hair was chocolate brown and curled at the nape of his neck. Looking down at my arm where he was still holding it, I mumbled an apology and quickly escaped before I fainted. I'll never forget how he smelled of Irish Spring soap. It smelled much better on him than on my dad. He had on an Atlanta Braves t-shirt and faded Levi's that were worn in all the right places.

I had always been painfully shy around boys. The only boyfriend I'd ever had up to that point had been in the fifth grade. His name was Chip Gun. I liked the arrangement where we claimed each other, but never spoke except through our friends or on the phone. We would send short, sweet notes to each other in class, or smile from a distance. *I like you; do you like me? Check yes or no.* I can still remember him chomping his gum through the phone lines on our nightly talks. His favorite was Bubble

Yum. We heard a rumor that Bubble Yum was made from spider webs. Of course, we still chewed it, daredevils that we were. We figured that was why you could blow such big bubbles.

Eventually summer break came, and we drifted apart. The next year, he had a new girlfriend; I moved on without a boyfriend, of course. In sixth grade, boys were becoming bolder and wanted something more than a silent girl to love from afar. I wasn't ready for face-to-face conversations—or for any hand holding, which was becoming quite the thing. Young couples would sneak and hold hands until a teacher scolded them but as soon as the teacher's head was turned, they were right back at it.

I had hoped by the time I was in high school my shyness would dissipate like a cloud of dust, but no such luck. I tried to talk to my sister about my anxieties, even then trying to form some kind of relationship with my only sibling, but it was no use. She was a senior and didn't have much use for what she called "silly boys."

I could always count on my mother for bringing me up when I was feeling blue, or giving me advice for whatever dilemma I was facing. She always had a smile on her face, and I never doubted her love for me. My father was more distant. I never knew where I stood with him, and wondered on many occasions if he even loved me. Sometimes I would catch him staring at me as if I was an enigma.

I was very different from my sister, Mary. She was tall and had a square chin like Maria Shriver. She also had hazel eyes, and the most beautiful head of thick, dark chestnut hair. It was naturally curly, and she usually wore it pulled back severely from her face. I was short—or petite, as my mom liked to say—with blond hair and blue eyes. I was small like my mother, but that was really the only resemblance. My mother said I looked like her sister Susan, who had died as a child of leukemia.

After my encounter with John that first time, I became obsessed. I was constantly looking for him in the halls or in the lunchroom. I knew he was an only child and that he played football. I knew who his friends were, and also the name of the girl who was usually hanging around him:

Trish Brown. Shelly, my best friend, told me Trish was his wannabe girl-friend. I couldn't help but feel jealous every time I saw her or any other girls with him. Sometimes, though, I would catch his eye and he would grin like he was remembering when I plowed into him. My face would turn red with embarrassment and my heart would beat wildly. My ninth-grade year finally ended, and summer was on the way; that's when life suddenly became more interesting.

Shelly's family belonged to the swim and tennis club in town and she would often invite me to spend the day at the pool. On the Fourth of July, we were lying there soaking up the sun when we heard some boys walk by us. I opened one eye, saw John, and immediately closed it again. Once they passed by, I elbowed Shelly and whispered excitedly, "There's John Carrier!" We both turned and watched them walk towards the pool and jump in, splashing each other. After a few moments, Shelly jumped up and exclaimed, "It's time for a swim!" Slowly I got up and walked behind her until we reached the edge of the pool.

Once we were wading in waist-deep water, we tried not to stare bla-tantly at the boys but took a few peeks, thinking they wouldn't notice. They were throwing a Nerf football back and forth in the pool. Shelly giggled and said, "Don't look now, but I think they're talking about us."

"What are you talking about?" Shelly nodded in their direction so I turned nonchalantly until I saw them. They were all standing there looking right at us, causing me to turn back quickly in embarrassment. I was sure they were probably talking about Shelly. We were both about the same size, but Shelly had at least one thing going for her that I didn't: a big bosom. It was hard not to notice her in her little bikini. I looked down at my one-piece suit, which was very modest and covered me in all the right places. "I think you're the one they're talking about."

"We'll soon find out; they're headed this way." Shelly stood a little straighter so that her chest was on full display.

I shook my head, wondering how she could be so obvious. She had no shame whatsoever...but that was Shelly, take it or leave it. My heart was racing and my face felt flushed. Sometimes I would develop ugly red splotches on my face and neck when I got nervous. *Please let this not be one of those times*! I thought. And sticking out my chest was not an option; looking pathetic would not help my cause.

Taking a deep breath, I turned and found John standing right next to me. He was smiling, his green eyes sparkling with mischief in the sunlight. He had a smattering of freckles across his nose, I noticed. "Hey, Josie. Trip anyone lately?" The other guys started laughing, and I wanted to crawl in a hole somewhere. A very dark, deep hole.

The best response I could come up with was, "Very funny." *He knows my name*! I looked at Shelly and she was trying not to laugh too, knowing the whole story of how I first ran into him. I gave her a dirty look until she looked almost apologetic, but didn't quite pull it off.

John laughed and said, "Just kidding. Are you guys coming to the cookout and fireworks?"

I nodded and Shelly said, "Yeah, my dad is in charge of grilling the hamburgers."

"Cool. We'll see you later, then." Our eyes lingered for a couple of seconds before John and the others turned and headed for the pool ladder. Shelly and I watched them as they walked towards the diving boards.

Once they left, I began fanning my flaming face. "Did that just happen? Did John Carrier actually talk to me and say my name?" And then more dramatically, "I can die happy now."

Looking down at her impressive cleavage, Shelly said, "He's pretty cute, but so is Steve." I didn't notice any of the other boys. I only had eyes for John.

Biting my nails in anticipation of the afternoon cookout, I wondered if I would be able to say something intelligent for once. Or would I act like a goober? I looked down at my non-existent cleavage and worried. My only hope was a miracle.

Later that afternoon, Shelly and I were sitting at one of the picnic tables eating our hamburgers when John and Steve, the boy Shelly was enamored with, sat down. John sat directly across from me and Steve sat across from Shelly.

They began telling us about the fireworks that were scheduled for later that night. Thankfully, Shelly's parents had already planned on staying, and I was going to spend the night with them. I could tell by the look on Shelly and Steve's faces that they already liked each other. His face kept dipping down, but it didn't seem to bother Shelly; it only made her stick her chest out even farther. When I looked at John, he was grinning. I couldn't help but smile back.

John said, "How old are you?"

God seemed to be listening to my earlier prayer because I managed to say, "Fifteen. I won't be sixteen until January. How old are you?"

"I'll be seventeen in January. When's your birthday?"

"January fifteenth."

"You're kidding! My birthday is January fifteenth!"

We both laughed. I thought he was teasing so I asked, "Your birthday is really January fifteenth?"

"It really is January fifteenth. Hey, let's make a date right now to spend it together. What do you want to do?" *Spend the whole evening looking into your dreamy eyes*, I thought. That's what I wanted to say.

Steve said, "You can go skiing! Beech Mountain has the best slopes."

I looked back at John and shook my head. I knew my parents would never allow me to go skiing with John. Did he think we were rich or something?

Shelly said, "Go to Lobster and More and get some crab legs. They have the best biscuits too!" Shelly began licking her lips just thinking of the warm, buttery garlic bread. Shelly had a weakness for bread, and it went straight to her chest.

I thought that would be nice but probably very expensive, so I sat quietly trying to think of something that would be appropriate and fun. I couldn't believe we were talking about a future date with John. I really only wanted to get through that day.

"I'm allergic to shellfish," John admitted with a sheepish grin. "How about bowling?" He looked so cute and adorable I would have said yes if he had suggested we ride around and bash mailboxes.

I'd only been bowling a few times with my church youth group and I'd had a lot of fun, even though I wasn't very good. "I'd like that."

"Great! It's a date then." I couldn't help but stare at John. He was so handsome and his eyes managed to draw you in until you fell deeper and deeper. I didn't tell him that January 15th was the perfect day. My parents wouldn't allow me to car date until I was 16, not that anyone had been asking.

After finishing our burgers, we all decided to go back to the pool and play football. Every time John threw the ball, I tried my best to catch it—but I missed it more times than I caught it. He laughed and told me I was hopeless and I threw like a girl. I said, "I *am* a girl!"

"I noticed." There was that grin again, the one that turned my insides to jelly and made my heart race. I couldn't remember having more fun in my life, and I wanted the day to last forever.

That night all four of us sat on Shelly's blanket watching the fireworks. Shelly and I sat in the middle with the boys on either side of us. Popping sounds like gunshots were getting louder and louder, punctuated with whirring high-pitched whistles. The acrid smell of smoke hung in the air. We were a little away from the main crowd, on a small hill close to the woods. I sat there amazed at the perfect symmetry of each display. You could hear people clapping and cheering as the displays got bigger and bigger.

"The fireworks are better this year." John turned to Steve and said, "Remember last year when Mr. Zucker almost had his hand blown off? I heard my dad tell my mom that he was drunk."

"Heck yeah! Someone started screaming because Mr. Zucker passed out when he saw all the blood dripping off his hand. That was so cool!"

Shelly said, "My dad said he lost his thumb. They found the stump, but it was too mangled to reattach."

"How horrible!" I exclaimed. "Is Mr. Zucker here this year?"

In a terrible English accent, Steve said, "Not bloody likely!" laughing hysterically at his own joke. I guess he thought that cussing made him look cool.

John shook his head and said, "He's not on the fireworks committee anymore. I think Mrs. Zucker put an end to that."

I couldn't get the image of poor Mr. Zucker's bloody stump out of my mind. I closed my eyes and hung my head between my legs. John placed his hand on my back. "Hey, are you okay?"

"I'm fine, just a little queasy."

Shelly laughed. "Josie has a weak stomach. One time, when we were hanging out at her dad's barn, the cat upchucked a half-eaten mouse. One minute Josie's standing there staring with her mouth hanging open, and the next she passes out. If I hadn't caught her, she would have fallen to the first floor."

I nodded and grimaced. "It was awful! I've never seen anything so disgusting! I swear I could see its little legs still moving. Oh, no! Let's talk about something else before I really do throw up."

The conversation turned to my family's farm. John said, "I'd give anything to live on a farm. I bet there's always something to do."

I couldn't believe anyone would actually *want* to live on a farm when you had a nice house in the city. "It's okay. The chickens and ducks are my favorite."

"You'll never guess what Josie's pet chicken is named: Helen the Felon! I'm sure you'll never guess why!"

Everyone laughed and I tried to explain. "She has a bad habit of pecking the other chickens' eggs, but she's the sweetest chicken ever. She runs to me and always wants me to hug her."

The fireworks were exploding in rapid succession, which indicated the end was near. It was loud and smoky as we all watched in awe. I didn't want the night to end. It was so perfect; *John* was perfect. We all lingered a little longer while the parents began cleaning up.

Shelly got up and said, "Steve and I will be right back. We're going to... um, see what kind of tree that is over there. I told him it was an oak, but he thinks it's a maple."

As they walked off, John and I looked at each other and laughed. Trying to come up with something to talk about, I blurted out, "What's your favorite class in school? I mean, if you have one."

Looking thoughtful, John said, "Probably shop class. Mr. Wallace is pretty cool. He's pretty laid back and lets us do what we want. I also like science. Ms. Kendall was tough in biology last year, but she always tried to make it interesting. What about you?"

Without hesitation, I blurted out, "Art, definitely art. I got an honorable mention in one of the art shows at the mall last year. It was a watercolor painting of a bluebird. They're my favorite birds."

John smiled. We sat in silence once again while the faint sound of "Born in the USA" played in the background.

John cleared his throat. "I knew you lived on a farm."

In shock, I looked at John. "Really? How did you know?"

"I was staying all night with my friend Chris, and I rode home with him on the bus. We were already in the back when you got on."

"Chris Dixon? His dad's farm is not too far from us. I don't remember you being on the bus."

"I do. It was the first time I ever saw you, and I thought you were pretty cute."

I tried not to smile but failed miserably. "This was before I ran into you in the hallway at school?"

John nodded.

Grinning, I said, "I was so embarrassed when I ran into you that day. Usually when I saw you in the hallway, there was some girl hanging around you." I didn't tell him I was always looking for him in the hallways. "Was she your girlfriend?"

"Trish? No, that's Steve's twin sister."

"So you think I'm pretty cute?" *Did I really just say that?* I could feel the heat crawling up my neck.

John was silent for a moment and then nodded slowly. "Yeah, that was before I got to know you."

My euphoric smile evaporated in an instant. "Excuse me?"

"What?" John raised his eyebrows and grinned.

"Before you got to know me? What's that supposed to mean?" I placed my hands on my waist for more emphasis.

"Well... I don't think you're cute anymore." John stood up and pulled me to my feet, holding both my hands. Looking down in my eyes, John's nose dipped down and touched mine. "I think you're pretty hot."

My legs almost gave out. *John Carrier thought I was hot! Good grief, I can really die happy now!* As his lips reached mine, my insides began to melt. Exhilaration took over my whole body while we stood there on that Fourth of July, kissing softly. It had to be the best first kiss ever.

Someone whistled and we jumped apart. Looking towards the woods, we saw Shelly and Steve walking towards us. Shelly's hair was all messed up and her clothes were a little askew. She had a sly look and was grinning at Steve. I knew I would hear all about it later.

Sometimes Shelly could really be outrageous, but her stories were always funny and entertaining. She had been kissing boys since kindergarten. She would chase them around the playground and show them her panties. Yes, she was one of *those* girls. Although we were as different as night and day, we were drawn to each other by our differences. I lived vicariously through her, and she seemed to need my reserved nature.

Shelly was never a favorite of my mother's. Shelly made the mistake of smarting off to her own mother on the telephone once when she was spending the night at the farm. Stupidly I tried it myself, but learned my lesson after I couldn't sit down for a week.

Thinking back to that day on the Fourth of July made me realize how different John's and my life had become. We were so in love in the beginning, and most of our married years were wonderful. How can two people start out so in love and end up like strangers? I wished John would look at me like he used to, like he thought I was special. I wished I could look at him with stars in my eyes, like I did when I was a teenager. We were more like brother and sister than husband and wife. It didn't happen overnight; it happened so gradually that we didn't even notice.

Chapter 3

I wiped the tears from my face, half expecting John to follow me to the bedroom but wasn't surprised when he didn't show up. *It would be nice if John cared enough to check on me and make sure I was okay.* In misery I lay back on the bed, wrapping myself around the pillow. The tears began anew and in exhaustion I fell asleep.

My cell phone vibrated waking me up. Matt, my oldest son had texted me. *Hey mom! Just got off work. Tyler and I are headed to the movies. Call you later.* I smiled and thanked God for Matt and Tyler. They shared an apartment together in Johnson City, Tennessee. Matt was a police officer, and Tyler attended the local university. They were the only reason I ever smiled anymore.

Remembering that I was supposed to sit with Dad for Mary, I pulled myself together, wrote a quick note to John, and quietly left the house. John was gone, probably out fishing at the pond or tinkering with something in the barn.

I found my dad sitting in his chair with a faraway look, the only look he had these days. He didn't even notice when I walked into the room. Mary was waiting with her pocketbook in hand, obviously annoyed that I was late. I didn't tell her why, knowing that she probably wouldn't care anyway.

"I've left his dinner warming on the stove. His stomach has been acting up, so please don't feed him anything else. I should be back around eight o'clock, nine o'clock at the latest." Without as much as a *hello, goodbye,* or *nice to see you,* she was out the door.

When I was sure she couldn't hear, I said in my most sarcastic voice, "It's nice to see you, too, Mary. No, it's not been such a great day. My life is falling apart but other than that, I'm just hunky-dory."

Feeling just a little bit childish, I walked towards the couch and sat down on the edge, looking at my dad. He immediately jumped up and began walking in circles around the living room. Somehow, he managed to not trip on all the pieces of old furniture scattered throughout the room. Every so often he would pause directly in front of me, look around vacantly, then turn around and begin walking again. This went on for about five minutes until he was tired and sat back down in his chair. Watching him this way broke my heart. Even though we were never as close as I would have liked us to be, I still loved him. Knowing that our chance had passed was something I would always regret. I always felt that I could have done more, tried harder, but I was too busy taking care of my own family.

Mary was his favorite. Mary seemed to understand him more than I ever could. They had more in common. For one thing, they both loved train sets. One of the bedrooms in the farm house was set up with a Lionel train set. They had been building a complete village that practically took up the whole room, working on it for years. They never included me.

One day when I was around eight years old, my mom found me sulking and asked what was wrong. I told her that I wanted to play with the trains too, but dad and Mary wouldn't let me. She hugged me and told me not to worry. "We'll sneak in there when they're gone sometime and we'll play with them all we want." We actually did a couple of times, but I accidentally broke one of the locomotives. I unhooked it and picked it up to look closely at it, but it accidentally slipped out of my hand. Dad and Mary both fussed and wanted to know what happened. Mom told Dad that she was cleaning in there one day and broke it herself. I never asked to go back, and she never volunteered to take me.

They weren't affectionate; I was. My mother loved my hugs, but Dad seemed to avoid them. The day my mother found out she had breast cancer was even more profound than it should have been because my father was already showing signs of Alzheimer's, and she didn't want to burden us with taking care of him. Poor, sweet, Mom fought with a vengeance, but in the end, she couldn't fight the disease that ravaged her body. The day she died, I felt as if my whole world had ended. There wasn't a day that went by that I didn't miss her like crazy; birthdays and holidays were the worst. The ache just wouldn't go away. I tried to deal with the pain the best I could, but my coping mechanisms hadn't turned out so well.

When Mom died, Mary eventually moved back in the farmhouse to take care of Dad as his disease got progressively worse. I tried to help at first, but with no encouragement from her or my dad it was easy to step back and let Mary do most of the work. Sometimes I think she enjoyed being the martyr. She wanted me to know about all the sacrifices she made and if I helped her more, she couldn't lord it over me.

I began to give up trying to understand Mary. Her personal life was a mystery to me. She was married at one time, but it didn't last very long. The only reason she gave was that they just didn't suit.

Thinking Dad might be hungry, I got his dinner and tried to feed him. At first, it was as if he had forgotten how to move his mouth but he finally began chewing the soft food. I prayed that he wouldn't get choked, or I would get an earful from Mary. She was so condescending sometimes. One time when Tyler was about six, he choked on some candy while in the back seat of the car. I panicked, of course. Luckily, he was okay. But of course Mary criticized my parenting skills, and said it was stupid when a mother could not perform the Heimlich maneuver on her own child. I guess she thought I should have gotten a nursing degree before I had kids.

I wondered where she was off to. She had been very secretive lately. I guessed it was none of my business; who was I to her but her only sister?

With nothing better to do, I began making up outrageous scenarios as to what Mary could be doing. Maybe she was meeting a secret lover, or maybe she was playing poker and was in debt up to her eyeballs. She would have to ask me to bail her out. I could just see her crying and saying, "I can't seem to quit! Help me, Josie, please!" That brought a smile because imagining Mary begging and asking me for help financially was just downright amusing. I hoped that whatever she was doing, she was having fun. After the last few months, we both needed some fun in our lives.

Taking up Dad's Bible I began to read aloud from the book of Job. It was always one of his favorite books, and it often fascinated me as well. Poor Job couldn't catch a break; he went from having everything to having nothing, but never doubted God's love and never lost faith. I wished I had Job's patience. I wished I could quit feeling sorry for myself and go about my day as if I was fine and nothing bothered me. At least I had a roof over my head, food to eat, and good health. Why couldn't I just appreciate that? Even though Mom was gone, the years we had were wonderful. And why did I need a husband who was crazy in love with me? Life happens, people change, and couples fall out of love.

Did I still love John? Yes, but there were no sparks anymore. Why did I need something more than what I had? Once upon a time, we had a great marriage. I missed it, and I missed the closeness John and I had once shared.

Well, do something about it then! I thought. It was my life, and life is what you make it. Moping around all the time didn't exactly make me attractive to John. I had lost all my aspirations, but it was time to get them back. Maybe if I had the sparkle back in my eye and a bounce in my step, John would do more than grunt and look through me.

I thought of how Mary used to always make fun of my dreams of becoming a famous artist. Delivering the mail was definitely not something that I had aspired to do back when I was younger. When did I stop painting? It was probably before the boys were even born. Real artists don't give up because they have children. John used to be so proud of my artwork. I remembered the painting I gave him on his 17th birthday; I had worked on it for months, and he was so surprised.

Chapter 4

After the Fourth of July, John and I saw each other a lot at the pool. Shelly, Steve, John, and I were having a great summer and enjoying each other's company immensely. I never told my parents because I knew they wouldn't approve. Shelly's parents were a bit more lenient, though. Shelly's mom would lay out by the pool with her friends all day, tanning, smoking cigarettes, and gossiping. She never concerned herself with what we were doing as long as we didn't aggravate her.

John never went beyond a few kisses and holding my hand, but Shelly said Steve had "happy hands" and was forever trying to touch her breasts. I wasn't surprised, since they were always on display at the pool. Instead of being offended, she would laugh and say, "It's what all the kids are doing, Josie." She then proceeded to tell me about a girl in the 11th grade who bragged about "doing it" with Todd Livingston at the movie theater while watching Jason hack a few teenagers to death in one of those *Friday the 13th* movies. I grimaced in disgust while Shelly laughed. I made a mental note to inspect my seat the next time I went to the movies.

By the time school began, John and I were definitely a couple—except for the fact that I still couldn't go out on an actual date with him. John and Steve were on the varsity football team, so Shelly and I would go to every home game and watch them play. I would always spend the night at Shelly's house on those nights so we could stay out later. She would tell her father to pick us up at the local pizza joint close to the school, where we would meet the guys after the game. John and I would share a ham and pineapple pizza, our favorite. I would listen intently as he talked about the game, thinking to myself how perfect he was. Steve would burp and spit pizza out of his mouth while Shelly giggled.

I couldn't wait until our birthday when I could finally go out on a real date with John *alone*. I had been working on painting his portrait for weeks, hiding it from my family. My art teacher helped me with a new technique that involved lots of bold color. It was different, but I liked it. My mom was surprised when I told her I had a date on my birthday. After asking me every question under the sun, she was finally satisfied and allowed me to go. January 15th turned out to be a very cold night, but thankfully the skies were clear and there was no snow predicted. John drove his mom's Oldsmobile, which had plush bench seats and sailed over the roads like a boat. After my mom grilled him about everything she could think of, she finally let us go and we headed to the bowling alley. Shelly and Steve had hinted around that they wanted to go too, but for once we ignored them and decided to go alone.

I was so excited and happy to be with John. I never knew that bowling could be so much fun, even though I lost every game. Every time it was my turn, I couldn't concentrate for wondering if John was looking at my behind. I had agonized over what jeans to wear, making sure I wore the ones that looked the best to accentuate every curve. Once I even turned around swiftly to see where he was looking and sure enough, his eyes were zoned right in on my butt. He looked up fast, trying not to smile. I gave him a dirty look and turned around before he saw my grin. The bowling ball went right in the gutter.

"Dadgummit!"

John laughed when I stomped my foot in frustration. With a smirk, John said, "You want to go to the kiddie lanes?"

"No, smarty britches! I'll get it next time." The next time I knocked most of the pins down, but left a couple on each side of the frame. I knew I was going to have to change strategies so when it was John's turn,

I decided I needed to clear my throat a few times. When that didn't seem to be working, I began coughing and then choking. I couldn't believe it when he got another strike.

"Yes!" John turned and sauntered back to his seat. "Nice try, Josie."

After knocking down five pins I came up with a better idea than choking myself to death. I walked back slowly and asked John for a drink of his soda. I slowly licked my lips and smiled a secret smile. After staring a few moments, I finally said, "It's your turn, John. Here's a kiss for luck." I bent down and placed my lips softly on his. Before he could open his mouth, I stepped back and whispered, "Luck."

"No fair, Josie." I could see John's Adam's apple move as he swallowed.

John got his first gutter ball after that. I couldn't help but smile to myself. I still lost each game, but didn't feel quite so bad about it. I learned a very important thing about John that day: With a certain look or touch, my big handsome boyfriend would become very flustered. It was thrilling and exciting knowing I had that power.

When it was time to go, we headed for the car. John opened the door for me and then got in on the driver's side. I started to ask him if he wanted to open the presents but before I could get the words out of my mouth, John leaned over and kissed me. Once our lips touched, John's mouth opened and I felt his tongue touch mine. Electric shocks shot straight through my body. I had never felt anything so wonderful and exciting.

I heard someone sigh as we pulled apart and realized it was me.

John whispered, "Happy birthday." He pulled a small box out of his jacket and handed it to me. I unwrapped it and was surprised to find a beautiful leather bracelet with my name on it.

"Oh, John, it's beautiful!" I put it on and it fit perfectly. I was so excited that I put my arms around him and hugged him.

I had almost forgotten about John's painting I was so dazed. When I finally remembered, I grabbed it from the back seat and handed it to him. All at once I was shy, scared that he wouldn't like it and embarrassed that it was probably a very stupid gift. If he didn't like it, he sure put on a good act.

"It's the nicest thing anyone has ever given me. I love it, Josie." I couldn't help but feel relieved. John carefully put the canvas in the back seat and turned towards me. Putting his arm around my shoulder, he pulled me closer and bent down towards my face. Once again, our lips met. Our kiss began slowly, gently, but soon turned more intense. I could hear John moan as he pressed harder and then felt his tongue once again slip in my mouth. I felt myself being pulled deeper and deeper as if we were melting into one body. John's hands were in my hair, twisting my face so he could get closer. We were both breathing heavily when the kiss ended.

"You can't imagine how long I've wanted to kiss you like that." John's hand was still on my face, caressing my cheek. "I guess we better leave if I'm going to get you home by ten o'clock." I could only nod because my mouth wasn't able to form the words to say anything.

All the way home, I couldn't stop thinking about John's kiss. As we pulled into our driveway, I was wondering if he would kiss me again. After John turned off the engine, he got out of the car and then came to my side and opened my door. We held hands as we walked to the side porch. I saw the curtains flutter in the kitchen window.

Shivering with cold, I turned and looked into John's eyes. "Thank you for a wonderful night, John. This has been the best birthday of my whole life."

John smiled. "Me too, Josie. I'll never forget it." John bent down and kissed me but it was almost like a feather, it was so light. I felt a little wanton because I wanted more, except that I knew someone was probably eavesdropping inside.

I watched him as he walked back to his car and smiled as he waved goodbye. As I walked into the house, I was grinning from ear to ear. Mom and Dad were watching television in the den, but Mom looked like the guilty party that had been spying on us.

The first thing dad said was "You're late."

"Only five minutes, Daddy."

"When I say ten o'clock, I mean ten o'clock." He turned back to the television as if the discussion was over, so I shrugged.

Trying to make up for dad's harshness, Mom said, "Did you have a good time, dear? John is a very nice young man."

"It was awesome, Mama! Look what he gave me." I put my arm out so she could admire my new bracelet.

After raising her eyebrows in surprise, she said, "Well, that was awfully nice. I'm glad you had fun."

I couldn't help the smile that spread across my face. I walked upstairs thinking I was the luckiest girl alive. That night I dreamed of laughing green eyes.

Chapter 5

Mary came home just before nine o'clock. I wasn't positive, but I thought I smelled cigarette smoke. Trying to make conversation, I asked, "Did you have a nice time?"

Hesitantly, Mary admitted that she did. "I had a very nice time." As if trying to explain why she needed a break, she continued, "Sometimes I just need to get out of this house, Josie. Being with Dad every day can really take a toll on you."

"I know Mary. I'm sorry. I wish I could do more."

"We really need to discuss what we're going to do. It's getting to the point that Dad's brain is forgetting to do the most basic functions. Pretty soon he won't be able to chew, swallow, or walk. We need to begin the process of finding a facility to take care of him. The Home Health nurse said it's time."

I knew that it would eventually come to this. Dad's disease had become progressively worse, especially since Mom died. I was guilty of putting it in the back of my mind, hoping that Mary would take care of it.

"We'll do whatever you think is best. I support you one hundred percent."

"I've already looked into a few nursing homes, and I think I've found the perfect facility. It's not too far, and I've heard good things from several of my colleagues. They have an opening in a couple of months."

"That's fine. Just let me know what I need to do."

As I walked back home, I thought about Dad and how horrible it was to be trapped like that in your own body. The closer I got home, the more nervous I got. What would I say to John after my outburst earlier that day? I don't know what I was worried about; it would be just like any other night. We would sit and watch television, and then go to bed without saying anything of substance. John would be thankful if I didn't say anything at all, as usual.

John wasn't in the cabin when I got home. I saw a light on in the barn so I decided to head that way and make John talk to me, whether he liked it or not. With determination, I began thinking of several ways to start the conversation. "John, we need to talk. I can't go on living like this anymore," or maybe "I think it's time for a vacation. We need to get away." This went on and on, but I couldn't come up with the right thing to say. I hoped the right words would come to me and said a quick prayer as I walked inside.

I heard John talking quietly, so I headed for his tool room. The closer I got, I realized that he was talking on his cell phone. His voice was gentle and tender, something I hadn't heard in a long time. My heart dropped and I knew right away that something wasn't right.

I stopped a few feet from the door, standing there in total shock. I could hear John say, "I know; I'm sorry. I'll try and find a way." My hands went to my face and I closed my eyes. "I have a job in Johnson City tomorrow. Maybe I can stop by on my way home."

I stepped up to the door of the tool room and pulled the door open. The phone was still at his ear but as soon as he saw me, he said, "I have to go," and hung up.

We stood there staring at each other for what seemed like hours instead of seconds. In that moment, I felt incredibly stupid. Suddenly I knew why John was so distant; everything fell into place. He was seeing someone else, just biding his time until he left me. Not an unusual story, but it happened to other people, not me.

John finally murmured, "What did you hear, Josie?" He was white as a ghost and looked incredibly guilty.

"I heard you talking to another woman. And apparently, you're going to stop at her house and see her on your way home." I really didn't hear much of the conversation, but I knew just by the tone of my husband's voice that he cared for whoever he was talking to. He'd always had a way of making me feel special, and it was like a punch in the gut to hear him speaking like that to someone other than me.

Shaking his head, John said, "I'm sorry, Josie... I didn't want you to find out this way."

Exactly how did *he want me to find out? Is there a better way to find out your husband's having an affair?* Maybe we could plan to have tea or coffee and discuss why he decided to fall in love with someone else. It could be the ten pounds I packed on since we got married, or maybe the extra wrinkles around my eyes, or the sagging skin at my throat.

All I could think to say was, "Who is it?"

John closed his eyes and took a deep breath. "I don't think that's important right now. Let's just talk..."

"Who *is* it, John? Tell me now!" My voice sounded loud and shrill in the quiet stillness of the barn. The roosting chickens began clucking and ruffling their feathers at the rude interruption. Ricky and Lucy jumped up nervously, pacing around our feet.

Knowing he couldn't get around it and I would find out eventually, John hung his head and whispered, "Shelly."

I stood there in total shock. "Shelly?" John nodded but wouldn't look me in the eye. "You and *Shelly?* Are you kidding me?!" John's hand went to his mouth, covering it in apprehension. "Look at me, John. You and Shelly, my best friend?" John finally looked at me and nodded once more.

Was this some kind of joke? I could remember a time when John didn't even like Shelly. He said she got on his nerves with her giggling, and she always wore too much makeup. She had always flirted with him, but I never dreamed he would return those feelings. Shelly flirted with everyone, for goodness sakes. It never meant anything—at least, that's what I had always thought.

31

John nodded, and I saw unshed tears filling his eyes. "Let me explain what I was trying to tell her."

I took a step toward John and slapped him with all my might. My hand stung and I could see his cheek turning red. The pain in his eyes was obvious, but he barely flinched.

In a voice that sounded a lot calmer than I felt, I said, "I heard you, John. I know exactly what you were trying to tell her, and I hate your guts. God help me, I hate you."

"I'm so sorry, Josie. Please listen to me."

I turned and walked slowly out of the barn, not wanting to hear any of his lies or excuses. Our love was dead. Our once perfect love was over, done, and in the past tense.

Chapter 6

I was falling hopelessly in love with John Carrier. He had to be the sweetest, kindest boy I had ever met in my life. Even Shelly was jealous of the way he treated me. She complained that Steve only wanted one thing, but apparently she didn't mind. We often went on double dates and I would cringe sometimes, wondering what was going on in the back seat.

One particular night we had gone to the Moonlight Drive-In. John's aunt and uncle worked there and always gave us free popcorn. They showed older movies, but it was always a lot of fun. As we sat watching *Cujo* terrorize a mom and her young son in their car, John had his arm around me and I had my head on his shoulder. We could hear lips smacking in the back seat and a lot of heavy breathing. John finally had enough and said, "Will you two cut it out?"

Shelly giggled and said, "Thank you, John! This guy is like an octopus!"

Steve groused, "When I get my license, you won't have to worry anymore."

"When you get your license, Shelly better turn and run!" I looked at John, so thankful that he respected me. Poor Shelly: maybe she would find a good guy like John too. Steve finally did get his license, but it wasn't long after that he and Shelly broke up. She told me that once Steve realized she wasn't going to give in to him, he told her he would find someone that would. She was upset, but soon set her sights on someone else. John told me that Steve said she was becoming too clingy and possessive. I figured they were both exaggerating.

John told me he was glad we didn't have to double date with Steve and Shelly anymore. The first time we were at a drive-in movie alone, John smiled and said, "Ahh...isn't it nice, not to have those two carrying on in the back seat?"

"Yes! I couldn't stand all that lip smacking. It was gross." I shivered and stuck my tongue out to emphasize my point. *Rocky* was playing, which wasn't the most romantic movie, but at least we were alone.

John started laughing and then grabbed me, kissing me all over my face while making loud sucking noises. I kept yelling, "Stop!" in between fits of laughing hysterically. I wasn't sure of the exact moment it happened, but the kisses went from being playful to something more passionate. One minute I was pushing him away, and the next I was pulling him closer. John groaned and started pushing me back until I was against the door and he was practically on top of me.

Realizing that we were going too far, I tried to get John's attention. "John... John." And then more loudly, "*John!*" He finally stopped, but his breathing was erratic. I noticed the windows of the car were beginning to fog up.

We both sat up and John looked a little sheepish. "Sorry, Josie. I'm as bad as Steve."

I was quiet, not sure of what I should say or do. My head was spinning, and it almost felt as if something had changed. It wasn't that I didn't want John, but certain ideals had been so ingrained in me that I couldn't just let them fly out the window. Besides, I was only 16, and not ready to take that next step.

I heard John say, "You're awfully quiet." I turned and found John looking at me. "Look, it's okay, Josie. I won't push you to do something you're not ready for."

In relief, I scooted over and put my head on his shoulder. I wanted to tell him it was okay, that I loved it when he kissed me. Instead, I took his hand and squeezed it.

John kissed the top of my head and put his arm around me. The scene where Rocky was chasing the chicken as part of his training routine came on. "You think Helen the Felon could make it in the movies?"

I snorted and then giggled out loud. I couldn't talk because I was laughing so hard. Popcorn spewed out of my mouth.

Nonchalantly, John took a napkin and wiped off the front dash. "Your chicken already has a cool name. She could give Rocky a run for his money." He pointed towards the big screen. "Rocky versus Helen the Felon... Don't forget to hide your eggs."

I looked at John and he had a smirk on his face. "You're real funny, John Carrier. Why would sweet Helen want to give up the country life? She has it made."

"But Hollywood could be calling. She could retire rich and live in luxury for the rest of her chicken days."

"She already lives in luxury. I even dig up worms for her."

"You dig up worms for a chicken?" John turned and put his hand under my chin. "You actually dig up worms for a stupid chicken?"

I looked horrified. "She's not stupid!"

Raising his eyebrows, John teased, "You might be a redneck if..."

"I'm not a redneck. I'm just very caring, and like to spoil my chicken."

John closed his eyes and shook his head. "So what does that say for me? My girlfriend likes to dig up worms for her pet chicken, named Helen the Felon. God help us all."

I smiled and batted my eyes. "How did you get so lucky?"

John pulled me close and hugged me. "I am lucky." After kissing my forehead, John said, "Luckiest guy in this car." My elbow accidentally punched him in the ribs. "Fine; luckiest guy in the drive-in."

"What?"

"Luckiest guy in Washington County?" Seeing the look on my face, he shook his head. "No? Okay, okay. Luckiest guy in the whole world, since the beginning of time."

"And don't forget it, mister." I crossed my arms and looked very smug.

"I just have one question. Do you have any other pets?"

I held up my hand and put my finger to my lips, thinking carefully. "Well, there's Sir Oinks-a-lot, Mr. Hasslehoof, and Vincent Van Goatie. They're all my pets, but I'm not as close to them as Helen. Oh! I forgot Clawsy! She's the barn cat, the one who likes to throw up mice."

John put both hands on his face and began rubbing his forehead. "I don't even know what to say, Josie."

I couldn't help but grin. "You can commend me on my very creative pet names."

John nodded. "Yes, I'll give you that. I've never heard anything like it."

"Do you have pets, John?"

John nodded slowly, but didn't say anything.

"Well? What is it, and what's its name?"

Shaking his head quickly, John said, "I'd rather not say."

"Oh, come on John! Tell me. Please? Please, please!" I begged and pleaded until he finally relented.

"It's a white teacup poodle, and her name is Precious. She was already named when Mom got her, and she wouldn't answer to anything else."

I sat in silence trying not to laugh. "That is just too much. John Carrier's dog's name is *Precious*." I sighed. "That's just...precious!" Then I was laughing so hard I snorted, but I didn't care.

"Go ahead. Laugh all you want, but Precious is anything but! That's the meanest dog that ever lived, and I've got the scars on my ankles to prove it."

I giggled off and on throughout the rest of the movie, thinking of bite marks on John's ankles.

Chapter 7

Could this really be happening? Was my husband really cheating on me with Shelly? How could they both be so cruel? I knew I was getting a migraine, so I went to the bathroom and took my prescription medicine. After shutting the blinds, I lay down on the bed and curled up in a ball. I'd been having a lot of bad headaches since my mama died. The doctor told me it was the stress. *Well, this sure isn't going to help.* So many questions were running through my mind. *When? Where? How long?* And most importantly, *why?* Knowing this wasn't helping my head, I tried to close my eyes and relax but then the tears began flowing. I heard a soft knocking on the door.

"Josie, can I come in?"

Before I could answer, John walked in and stood next to the bed. I rubbed my temples and ignored him. Maybe he would take the hint and go away. It was so quiet I could hear the wall clock ticking and his breathing. It was labored, as if he had run a marathon. After taking a shaky breath, he said, "I'm sorry, Josie. I didn't mean for it to happen...it just did. Ever since your mom died..."

"Don't you *dare* blame this on my mama!" I tried to yell, but it came out as a whisper. I held my head, trying to stop the stabbing pain.

"I'm just saying that you've been different since then. I felt as if you didn't love me anymore. I got lonely; Shelly was there. I wish I could take it back, but I can't. I knew it was a mistake when it happened, and I've been trying to tell her that."

I slowly turned my head and looked up at him with disgust. To blame my dead mother for his discretion was more than I could take. If I'd had the strength to stand up, I would have; I also would have punched him until he hurt as bad as I did. Instead, I turned away from him and hugged the pillow to my chest. "Just go away. I just...I just can't right now."

Instead of leaving, John sat at the end of the bed. I could hear him breathing slowly through his nose, exhaling with a shaky breath. The ticking of the clock was getting louder and louder. Even the rustle of the comforter was maddening. Every sound was amplified until I couldn't stand it anymore.

I whispered, "Do you love her?" By this time my head was pounding so hard I felt as if I was going to throw up again, but I had to ask that one question. I just couldn't leave it alone.

John shook his head. "No. I love you." He looked sad. He looked contrite.

It made no difference. To know that someone I had loved almost my whole life betrayed me in such an intimate way, with my best friend, was beyond comprehension. Life would never be the same. I would never be able to look at John the same way again. I knew things had been different with us, but I had assumed that we would get past it. I knew that eventually I would begin healing and John would be there for me, just like always. I was so wrong. While I was mourning my mother, John had turned to someone else. John and Shelly... It was inconceivable, unthinkable, unbelievable, and absolutely ludicrous. And yet, it was a fact; it was now my reality. Nothing could change it. Ever.

"How could you do this to me...to us." John reached for my leg but I jerked it away, making my head feel like it was being split in two. I couldn't control the bile that rose to my throat and in humiliation I rolled over and threw up in the trashcan I had left next to the bed. The pain in my head and heart was so bad that at that moment I didn't care whether I lived or died. With all the effort I could muster, I whispered, "Just leave...I can't deal with this right now."

We both stared at each other. I could see pain and regret in John's eyes, his beautiful green eyes that just broke my heart into a million pieces. I slowly rolled over on the bed until I was facing the wall, dismissing him.

I heard John go the bathroom to get another trash bag. He turned on the bedside lamp and then removed the soiled bag from the can. I could feel him watching me silently from the door until wordlessly leaving the bedroom.

I tried to relax so the pain would ease up. The tears slid down my face, puddling on my nose and the pillow case. God help me, what was I going to do now? The only person I could turn to, the only person who could help me, was dead. Buried. Gone. I tried to imagine her sweet face. I pretended she was beside me, rubbing my back, consoling me in the special way mothers have. I could even imagine her scent surrounding me along with all of her love, comforting me so that I wouldn't fall apart. "What am I going to do, Mama?" I tried to pray, but all that came out was a whispered, "Help me!"

In the dim light, I looked at our photographs on the wall, taken in happier times. In every photo, the love we shared was unmistakable, written in plain sight on our faces. One of my favorite pictures was of John in his cap and gown, with his arm around me. We were so happy and in love.

Chapter 8

John had just graduated high school, and I had finished my junior year. Although John was going to go to the community college close by, I still worried that he would tire of dating a high school girl when he could date someone older and more sophisticated. Although John had let it be known that he was ready to take our relationship a step further, I was still holding myself back. John told me he would wait until I was ready, but I could tell he was becoming very frustrated.

Shelly told me it was no big deal. "Just make sure you use protection. Getting pregnant can ruin everything." The most exciting thing that had happened at our high school that year was when Natalie Cooper got pregnant. It was surprising because Natalie was a cheerleader and very popular. If it could happen to her, it could happen to anyone. I'm sure the hanky-panky at Jefferson High was curtailed that year thanks to Natalie. I know it influenced me.

That summer, my dad hired John to work at the farm. It was great having him around all the time. Sometimes, after my chores were done, I would hang around the barn just to be near him. I loved riding the tractor with him or helping him mend the pasture fences. My mom was as crazy about John as I was. He had more meals at our house than he did at his own because Mom was always inviting him to stay.

Mary had never had a serious boyfriend; she'd only been on a few dates. She was in her final year at the community college and planned on becoming a registered nurse. She still lived at home while going to school full-time and working part-time in the emergency room. To her credit, she was nice to John and treated him better than she treated me. John always worked hard and my dad was glad to have the extra help.

One Saturday, my parents had gone to an auction to sell some cattle and Mary was working at a local emergency clinic. John had been cleaning and straightening out the barn in the upstairs level. Years ago, it was used for hanging tobacco to dry. Since we didn't farm tobacco anymore, it was mostly used for storage and hay for the cows. Critters liked to sneak around and cause all kinds of messes. Snakes, opossums, rats, mice, and raccoons were always a nuisance in a barn looking for random chicken eggs, feed or anything else they could find. In the springtime, birds would be flying around the barn in abundance, nests in all kinds of places. Carpenter bees, wasps, and hornets would sometimes buzz so loud you could feel the whole barn vibrating.

My Saturday chores would consist of cleaning the house, doing a load of laundry or two, and feeding the chickens and pigs. It was lunchtime, so I decided to take John something to eat. I found him knocking some old wasps' nest down from the rafters and decided to watch him for a moment before he knew I was there. I couldn't help but admire the muscles rippling in his arms. John sensed my presence and turned. I smiled. "I brought you some lunch. Are you hungry?"

"Sure." John put the pitchfork down and walked towards me. Taking the glass of tea, he gulped it until it was almost gone.

"It's a roast beef sandwich." After handing him the sandwich wrapped in a kitchen towel, I walked over to the doorway overlooking the farm and sat down. John followed me and sat beside me, our feet dangling over the edge. When he finished his sandwich and the rest of his tea, he wiped his face and mouth with the towel. I took it from him and threw it over my shoulder.

"Thanks, Josie. I was getting hungry." John lifted my hair braid and rubbed it between his fingers. He had always loved my hair, and begged me not to cut it. It was thick but fine, hanging almost to my waist. I had fair skin and freckles on my nose and cheeks. "You know, I was thinking about you right before you showed up."

"You were? What were you thinking?" I smiled and took the hat off of his head and placed it on mine.

"I was thinking about how hungry I was and hoped you brought me some lunch." John had a smirk on his face. "And there you were."

"What if I hadn't showed up, Mister Hungry as a Horse?"

"Well, I guess I'd starve to death and think what a lazy girlfriend I had." John grinned.

I harrumphed and put my hands on my hips. "I was working too, you know." When his eyebrow raised mockingly, I playfully punched him in the stomach.

Letting out an exaggerated oomph, John grabbed me, took off his hat and rubbed his knuckles on the top of my head. I yelled for him to stop and pushed him as hard as I could. Jumping up, I ran. I could hear John coming after me and slowed down just a little so he could catch me. I backed up against the barn wall and said, "I'm sorry, John. I didn't mean to punch you."

John began walking slowly toward me with a sly smile. "Yes, Josie, you did."

"No, seriously! You know me and my temper. Sometimes it gets the better of me." I was trying not to laugh.

"What do you think your punishment should be?"

"Punishment?" My eyes opened wide, and I fluttered my lashes to my best advantage.

"Yes. Punishment." John stopped right in front of me and placed both hands on the wall above my head.

I swallowed deeply. "Nothing too bad. It's not like you didn't do anything to deserve it."

"What? That I was 'hungry as a horse?'" John bent down, his mouth close to my ear. I could feel his warm breath.

I closed my eyes in anticipation. "Well, I thought that was a clever description...since you were so hungry and all." I whispered. I felt John's lips on my neck and gave him more access by turning slightly. I placed my fingers in the belt loops of his pants and pulled him in.

John's hands cupped my face and he leaned down to kiss me. My head was spinning as our mouths opened and our tongues danced. My legs felt weak and almost gave out.

John whispered, "I love you, Josie, and I'm 'hungry as a horse' for you."

I giggled. Smiling, I said, "That hungry, huh? Well, I love you too." John wrapped his arms around me and we held each other close, savoring the moment. "If this is my punishment, maybe I should be bad more often."

"Be bad all you want, baby." I felt his lips on the top of my head.

We both heard the sound of Dad's farm struck at the same time and pulled apart.

"Guess I better get back to work." John kissed me quickly one more time and then walked away. He was a little intimidated by my father, and never wanted to be caught in any compromising positions whenever he was around.

Taking a few deep breaths, I picked up his tea glass and slowly walked out of the barn with a silly grin on my face. Mom and Dad were getting out of the truck. "Any luck at the auction?" We kept a few cattle to graze our land. Money my dad made on cattle would always help with the expense of the farm.

Dad walked to the bed of the truck to get some chicken feed out of the back. "We made a good profit on those young heifers. Where's John? I need to tell him tell him where I need those chicken coop repairs."

As he headed for the barn with the feed tossed over his shoulders, I said, "Upstairs."

Mom took my arm as we walked towards the house. "How's John today? Your father's been bragging on what a fine job he does working around the farm."

I grinned. "He's great. I just took him some lunch." I tried to suppress the sheepish grin on my facing remembering John kissing me and telling me he loved me.

My mom smiled. "Tell him he's welcome to stay for dinner. I'm making chicken and dumplings tonight. I know how much he loves them."

"I'll tell him." We walked into the kitchen and I began cleaning up the mess from making John's lunch. "There's supposed to be a meteor shower tonight and since it's supposed to be so clear, a bunch of us are going to the river to watch them." I put the tea and mayonnaise in the refrigerator and stood there with the door open, letting the cool air of the refrigerator fan my hot face.

"Where are you going to watch them?"

I shut the door and went to the sink. I wet the wash cloth and began wiping the counter. "Down at the swinging bridge."

After a short silence, I looked up at my mom. "Is that okay?"

She nodded. "I know that things are pretty serious between you and John. Am I right?"

I nodded back at her. "Yes." I was a little embarrassed, and didn't say anything else.

She took my hand and smiled. "I just want you to be careful. I was young once and I know how easily things can get out of hand if you're not careful." Squeezing my hand a little she said, "Just don't put yourself in a situation where that can happen."

I knew my face was red. "I won't, Mama. I promise." At least I would try my best.

"You know how much I like John, but I know he's a little older. Sometimes boys won't think about the consequences because they're not thinking clearly." I tried to pull away but she held my hand tight. "I know this is uncomfortable to talk about, but I need to make sure you understand." She took her other hand and lifted my chin so I would look her in the eye. "If he loves you, he will wait."

I nodded, embarrassed beyond words. She took the wash cloth from me. "Now go on, and enjoy your day. I'll finish up the house."

I turned to go but at the last minute, I turned and hugged her. "I love you, Mama."

"I love you, too, darling. You're my pride and joy."

The rest of the afternoon, I worked on my oil painting of the river. I wanted to be able to not only see the rippling current, but to hear it as well. I placed an egret in the water, its stance majestic and regal. The sun peeked through the silver birch trees swaying in the breeze, their leaves sparkling like shoots of fire. Except they didn't look like shoots of fire. Far from it. I put down my brush and carefully laid the canvas on an old sheet. I hugged my knees and closed my eyes and tried to imagine the sounds of the water and leaves blowing in the wind. I pictured the egret flapping its wings, beginning to lift off of his skinny legs and fly to another babbling brook where he might have more luck catching dinner. I decided I would have more luck if I went to the river myself.

I packed all of my painting supplies and walked to my favorite spot. It was shady enough to be cooler, and the perfect river rock sat quietly waiting for my behind to sit on it. Instead of painting, I decided to just enjoy the moment. My mind wandered to my earlier conversation with my mother. I knew John loved me, but did he love me enough to wait? I knew that if I let him, we would have definitely moved on in our relationship. He had no idea how much I wanted to, how tempted I was.

Later that night I was walking down the swinging bridge with John behind me stomping his feet so that I swayed back and forth. "Cut it out! If I fall over, you're the one that's going to have to retrieve my dead, broken body." I gave him a pointed look as I held on tight to the skinny rails.

John rolled his eyes. "I don't think you'll drown. It's only two feet deep here."

"Exactly! My head will hit one of those rocks and crack like a watermelon."

"At least the fish will have a good dinner."

I stopped and turned, shoving the blanket in his arms. "Try stomping now. Maybe you'll fall over and feed the fish." I continued walking until I got to the steps at the other end surveying the area to find the best place to watch the meteor shower.

John began gathering wood from the riverbank to make a fire for roasting marshmallows; that would also help deter the mosquitoes. "How many are coming? I'll find some sticks for the marshmallows too."

"Let's see." I began counting with my fingers. "Me and you, Shelby and Mark, and Kristy and Brian. That's all I know for sure."

"Chris and a couple of his buddies are coming too, since it's on his dad's property."

"Get at least ten. If it's not enough, they can get their own." I spread the blanket out and set down the bag I had been carrying. Besides marshmallows, it contained some bug spray, which I immediately applied liberally to my skin and clothes. I watched John play with the fire until it began smoking and finally emitted some small flames. Of course the smoke drifted right in my face, making me cough. Waving my hands in front of my face, I said, "Good grief. And don't you say it."

"Say what?" John grinned, enjoying my discomfort. "You know it's true; smoke follows beauty." He threw some dried leaves on the fire, which caused even more smoke. "You see it doesn't follow this ugly mug."

"Well, beauty doesn't mean a thing if you smell like smoke." I got up from the blanket and moved to a smoke-free zone. I put my hands on my hips and asked, "So, what do you think of Mark? Shelby is excited about going out with him. Is he a good guy?"

"He's a pretty good guy. I've played football with him since the sixth grade."

"What do you mean, 'pretty good?'"

"He's fine! He's the one that should be worried."

"What do you mean?"

"Well, she's a little obsessive." After seeing my inquiring look, he said, "I've heard some talk."

"Who said that? I know she's a little obsessive. The guys are really talking about it? Who?"

"Oh no. Not going there." John shook his head to emphasize his point. Luckily for him, we heard some commotion on the bridge. We looked up and saw the rest of the gang, the bridge swaying heavily with so many people on it. Kristy and Shelly were followed by the rest of the boys.

Chris had brought his guitar, so I knew we were in for a treat. The whole evening was a blast. By the time the meteor shower began, we were all lying down on the blankets to watch the sky in awe. I was beside John, and we were holding hands. I noticed Mark had his arm around Shelly, but she was looking at John, not Mark. When she saw me looking, she smiled. It wasn't the first time I had caught her studying John with a wistful look in her eye. She always told me she wanted a relationship like John and I had. I smiled back and winked at her. I knew I was lucky. Not everyone had what John and I had. Maybe Mark would be 'the one.' Shelly smiled and then turned towards Mark, placing her cheek on his chest.

Chapter 9

My migraine was so bad that I couldn't get out of bed for two days. Slowly I started coming back to life, but reality hit me hard. I wanted to stay under the covers so I wouldn't have to face it. I knew I was just delaying the inevitable, so I finally got out of bed that Wednesday morning, called work again, and told them I would be back the following day. John was working a job somewhere. Working the farm full-time did not pay all our bills, so he worked as an electrician by day.

I wouldn't let myself think about Shelly before, but now I began wondering when and where their affair began. There must be a clue somewhere. Shelly was a hairdresser and had her own shop in town. She had been divorced twice and had one daughter, Carly, who was the same age as our youngest, Tyler. They were attending the university together. Our oldest, Matt, had just graduated from the same university before he got his job at the police department.

Maybe Shelly had asked John to do some work for her at her house or her business. I could just imagine her sticking out her big boobs, trying to call attention to the only thing she had going for her. John had always liked the natural look, and Shelly was anything but. She wore her clothes too tight, teased her platinum blonde hair, and wore outrageous colors and too much makeup. I looked at my nails, which I had chewed on until they were a mess, and thought about Shelly's perfectly manicured nails. I still had the same dirty blond hair, but it needed a good trim. I had put on a little weight, but it wasn't as if I was fat. My wardrobe was pathetic, though. Delivering mail didn't require anything fancy, just comfortable. I figured I would be the perfect candidate for someone's fabulous makeover show on television.

The image of John and Shelly kissing popped into my head and almost brought me to my knees again. How could they do this? I felt so betrayed and terrified of what was ahead. Knowing I couldn't be there when John got home, I started packing my things. I would stay in my old room at the farmhouse with Mary. I dreaded telling her what John had done, but knew it was inevitable. Feeling weak and exhausted, I lugged everything I needed to my car.

Dad's nurse was surprised to see me carrying in all of my things. Looking like death warmed over, I mumbled, "I'm going to be staying here for a while." Once I was settled in my old room, I decided to lie down on the bed and give in to the exhaustion that had threatened to overwhelm me all day. I hadn't left a note for John, knowing he would see my car parked in front of the farmhouse when he came home from work. He didn't deserve any consideration from me after what he had done. I hoped he was miserable knowing he broke up our marriage. Sleep came soon, but my dreams were overwhelming. In them John and Shelly were standing arm in arm while I watched them, crying, "Why?" Shelly's smirk and John's indifference told me all I needed to know.

It was almost dark when I finally woke up. I walked into the living room. Mary was sitting on the couch, watching the news on television, and Dad was in his chair staring into space. "John called. He wanted to make sure you were okay."

"What did you tell him?"

"I told him the truth: that I didn't know. What's going on, Josie?"

Here we go, the part I dreaded; telling the people I love that my husband is having an affair and that my marriage is over. Taking a deep breath, I said, "It's over. I found out John is having an affair with Shelly." Mary actually looked shocked as I sat down on the couch. I wiped away the tears that wouldn't stop coming.

Mary was never a big fan of Shelly's; but, like me, I'm sure she never imagined that Shelly would sleep with her best friend's husband. Handing me a box of tissues, Mary said, "I don't believe this. Are you sure?"

"Yes, things have been off for a while. I caught him talking to her on the phone last night, and he admitted it. Mary, what am I going to do?" Pulling my knees up I buried my face and put my arms around my legs. Feeling my head start to pound, I tried to relax. "I've had a migraine since Sunday night."

"This is crazy. John is the last person I would ever have thought capable of cheating. Have you taken your medication?"

I nodded and said, "He said I've been different since Mama died, like it's all my fault." Looking up, I said, "Do you mind if I stay here for a while?"

"If that's what you want." Mary sat there in silence, shaking her head, and eventually turned back to the news.

I took a tissue out of the box and blew my nose. Leaning my head back, I thought of Mama and wished she was there. She would know exactly what to say, and whatever it was would make me feel better. Her arms would be around me, comforting me; her words would soothe and calm me. I looked down and there was a small pillow on the end of the couch. I remembered when Mom had stitched the Bible verse on it; *Be still and know that I am God,* I read. I picked it up and hugged it to my body, feeling closer to her immediately.

After the news ended, Alex Trebek's voice gave the answers on the television while the contestants asked the correct or incorrect questions. Mary knew almost all of the questions. I kept quiet, knowing it annoyed Mary when you talked during one of her favorite shows. During the commercial break I asked her, "Mary, have I been blind? Have you ever noticed anything between Shelly and John?"

"Of course not, but I haven't been looking." She got up from her chair and headed towards the kitchen. "Want any tea?"

I nodded my head. "Sure. I'll take some Earl Grey, if you have it." I hugged my pillow tighter, listening to Mary rummage through the kitchen. Once the kettle was on the stove, she walked back into the living room. The commercials were over so I sat in silence once again. Mary rattled off all the questions until the next commercial began and walked into the kitchen as the kettle started whistling.

Mary hollered, "Do you want honey or sugar?"

"Honey, please."

"One teaspoon or two?"

"Two."

Carrying out the teacups, Mary handed me one with steam still rolling off the top. I tried to take a sip but decided to blow on it instead. I thought of all the times my mother and I had shared a cup of tea over the years. I felt her presence all around me and savored the moment. The music signaling the final answer began playing, Mary looking pleased. "What is *Cat on a Hot Tin Roof?*"

I looked at my sister, amazed. "How do you know all the answers?"

Mary picked up her teacup. "You mean questions?" She took a careful sip. "I don't know. I've always been able to remember useless trivia. It's not a big deal."

I shook my head. "Well, I'm lucky if I remember my name." I held the cup in my hands enjoying the soothing smell and warmth. "I really appreciate you letting me stay here. I don't know what's going to happen. I just can't think past the shock right now."

Mary was silent but she nodded. She picked up the remote and searched through the channels. After finding an old *Law and Order* rerun, she put the remote back down to watch the program.

"I just can't believe it...John and Shelly."

Again, Mary remained silent, watching the show intently.

"It's absolutely crazy. I never would have guessed it in a million years." Realizing it was pointless trying to converse with Mary, I gave up and focused on my tea. Mary didn't care and had no opinions. Might as well keep my mouth shut.

I wondered what John was doing. Was he watching television, or tinkering in the barn? Was he feeling bad or relieved? Would he go to Shelly, now that it was out in the open? Would she rub it in my face? Once again, I began searching through my memories for any sign of them becoming closer.

Chapter 10

It felt as if I would never graduate high school. John was busy at school and Shelly once again had a new boyfriend she was enamored with, so to pass the time, I devoted myself to painting. I was always outside somewhere, my easel propped up, painting different scenes around the farm. I especially loved the spring when wildflowers were popping up all over, creating beautiful colors at every turn. I didn't limit myself to just landscapes because the pigs, cows, and chickens were fun to paint as well. I loved to paint the proud rooster as he ruled his hens, or the bull staring at me with curiosity as he chewed fresh grass, all the while his tail swishing back and forth to bat the summer flies.

One beautiful spring day, I was painting the pond and admiring the way the sun glistened off of the water. I was so intent on getting the colors just right that I didn't even notice I wasn't alone until I felt John's hands on my shoulders. Jumping, I turned my head and saw John grinning. I yelled, "You scared me to death!"

John was laughing as he put his arms around me. Leaning back, I closed my eyes and said, "I've missed you."

"It's only been a few days." His hands started massaging my shoulders and then went down to my waist. When they began inching their way back up, I sucked in my breath as they stopped just below my breasts.

"What are you doing, John?" I tried to keep my voice even so he wouldn't know how much he was affecting me.

"You look so tempting sitting here. I just want to kiss you a little." John walked around my stool, taking the paintbrush out of my hand and placing it with the rest of my art tools. Pulling me against him, he took my lips quickly, causing my head to spin out of control. He tasted of warm sunshine and peppermint. Between breathless kisses, John whispered, "Mmm, you taste so good. Have you been chewing the wild mint?"

I nodded. "Yeah. It's all over the creek."

John smiled and pulled me closer. "I've missed you so much this week. It's been crazy with my finals coming up"

"I've missed you too, John." I was reveling in the wonderful feel of John's arms wrapped around me, listening to the woodpecker pecking on the hollow dead tree still standing in the pond. "I can't wait until I graduate. I hate school without you there. Guess what? Sally has a new nest. We may have some sweet little ducklings soon." My hands ran down his arms and then around his waist. "I've been checking on them a lot. I'm afraid something will get into the nest like they did last time. Probably a raccoon."

"You can't watch them all the time. That's just part of nature." John took my hand and we began walking in the shaded path that ran along the creek bed.

"But Sally would be such a good mom." It was warm and dragonflies were swooping around our heads. The blackberry vines on the trails were blooming, but without a lot of sun they wouldn't have much fruit. The wonderful smell of jasmine tickled our noses and the crackle of last year's fallen leaves crunched under our feet.

"How's school? Is your political science class any better?"

"It's okay. I'm doing better than I was. What about the art show? You got anything in it?"

I squeezed John's hand and said, "Yes! Mrs. Gunter loved my recycled art piece, the one with all the stuff I found around the barn. We should have the results of the show when we come back from spring break."

"That's good."

We walked in silence up the trail next to a small waterfall, which was running fast due to some recent heavy rains. We had to walk around some mud and jump over the trail in a few places where the water rushed down. John picked up a couple of branches that had fallen across the rocks.

As we reached the top I said, "How's your grandma?" John's grandfather had died right before Christmas and his grandmother was having a rough time. Everyone had to take turns staying with her because she kept having panic attacks.

"She's a little better. Mom said she hadn't had an attack in a while. My cousin Emily moved in with her, at least until the end of summer."

"I'm so glad. I know Emily will be good company for her."

John stopped suddenly and looked up. "There it is!"

I looked up and sure enough, the eagle was right above us. It was so beautiful and majestic. We would often see it flying up and down the river, too.

John took my hand and helped me cross a muddy spot. "I wonder if its nest is around here."

"Maybe. Dad said he thought it was, but who knows?"

"See any coyotes lately?"

"Actually, I saw a mother and her pups. I was walking with Red and he started barking at something." Red was Dad's old coon dog. "He took off running and I saw something up on the hill. Red must have realized what it was at the same time I did, and began running back towards the barn. I took off too, and didn't look back. I didn't know I could run that fast."

"You need to carry a gun if you go walking. I worry about you."

"I know. I just don't think I could shoot it."

"You could if you thought it was going to eat you."

"Yeah. Maybe." I bent down and picked up some wild mint growing next to the water. I put a piece in my mouth and gave some to John. "The Dicksons said they saw a bear come out of the woods, cross the river, and go up into the mountains across the road."

"That's it. You need to either get a gun or stay off the trails."

"You sound like Mom. I can't go anywhere without her ringing that stupid bell." There was an old bell on the back porch that my mom would ring whenever lunch or dinner was ready, and also when she wanted me to come home. If I didn't show up quick enough, she would send Dad after me. I usually got an earful after that.

John laughed. "Yeah, she sure won't let us stay out here long without ringing it."

"Speaking of, I guess we better head back before she fires it up."

John took my hand and we headed back down the trail. "Did Shelly tell you she showed up at our dorm?"

"What?"

"Yeah."

"No, she didn't tell me. Between Todd and her new friend Carol, we haven't talked a whole lot." I stopped when I saw some pretty spring flowers on the path, gathering them in a bunch for a vase. "Was Carol with her?"

"Does she have red hair?"

"Yep. That's her. She's very cute, but a little on the wild side."

"That's definitely her." John rolled his eyes.

I laughed. "Did they flirt with you?" I handed him a flower. "When I talk to Shelly all she can talk about is Todd, Todd, Todd. I'm surprised she's out and about without him."

John placed the flower I gave him next to my ear and swept my hair away from my face. "God, you're beautiful, Josie." Pulling me close, he whispered, "I don't know what I would do without you. I love you so much."

I put my hands on each side of John's face. "I love you too, John." We kissed once more and then headed back towards the house. "I'm sorry if Shelly and Carol were being a nuisance. Things must not be going very well with Todd." I knew that Shelly was frustrated. She just couldn't seem to find the right guy. Her relationships always ended badly. I felt sorry for her. And now it didn't look like Todd would last either. "Maybe there's someone at school you could set her up with?"

"Absolutely not!"

"Well, I don't like her hanging out with Carol so much. She's a bad influence." I had heard rumors, but Shelly insisted that they weren't true.

"That's her problem. And she can find her own boyfriend! I don't want to talk about Shelly anymore. Let's talk about how cute you look in those little shorts." John raised his eyebrows and grinned.

I looked down and grinned. "What? This old thing?" I shrugged and said, "Daddy says they're too short."

"Your daddy is right. They're absolutely too short to wear around anyone but me." Placing his hands on my behind, John pulled me close. "They make your sweet butt look mighty fine."

I put my arms around his neck. "I'm glad you think so, Romeo."

Before we could kiss again, the bell began ringing.

Groaning, John's head fell back.

"Saved by the bell!" I laughed and began walking back towards the pond and my art supplies. If John acted a little distracted that day, I didn't notice. Looking back, I had a sinking, horrible suspicion about John and Shelly.

Chapter 11

Going back to work helped take my mind off constantly picturing John and Shelly together. I thought I would go crazy imagining the man that I loved since I was 15 being with someone else. Delivering the mail was something I had done for so long that it wasn't much of a challenge. My route was easy; people didn't move around a lot in the country. The money was good, and it helped put my boys through school. Matt had wanted to work in law enforcement since he was a little boy. Matt was always the cop and Tyler was always the robber when they played. Tyler still wasn't sure what he wanted to be, but I was betting he would follow in his big brother's footsteps. Unlike Mary and me, Matt and Tyler were always close. I knew it would kill them to find out that their parents' marriage was over. I dreaded telling them, and decided to put it off as long as I possibly could.

As I approached Mrs. Jenkins house, one of my favorites on my route, I saw her sitting on her front porch. We had developed a close relationship, especially since my mom died. She was close to 80, but feistier than most people my age. Less than five feet tall, Mrs. Jenkins probably didn't weigh 90 pounds soaking wet. She always made me smile, even in my foggiest moments. I pulled in her driveway, got her mail together, and walked to the porch.

"Hey, Mrs. Jenkins, how are ya today?" I put her mail on the little table and sat down in the rocker beside her. I noticed right away that her tightly curled hair was a little bluer than usual.

"Bring us some tea, Bert!" Bert was her husband. He didn't say much but was as sweet as could be: a little strange, but sweet. He had retired a few years before after being a mortician most of his life.

"Where've you been, girl? I've been worried sick."

"I had a migraine...couldn't get rid of it." I didn't want to look at her because she had an uncanny way of guessing the truth in any situation. I knew that before I walked off of her porch, she would know everything.

"Thank the good Lord yer back! I been gettin' that hussy Melva Turner's *True Story* magazines. Jack Hess must deliver the mail with his eyes shut." Mrs. Jenkins shook her head and rolled her eyes. "Seems to me that yer migraines are brought on by stress, young'un'. What have you got to be stressed about? You and yer young feller have a fight?"

I rolled my eyes. "Something like that."

"Want to borry my whoopin' stick?" The thought of that made me giggle for the first time since Sunday. "I can make some of my special brownies for him and he wouldn't come out of the crapper for a few days." Mrs. Jenkins leaned in closer and whispered, "Never hurt Bert."

"That sounds... He's pretty deserving of it, but no." Bert came out with our iced tea. I gulped it down, realizing I was thirstier than I thought. "Thanks, Bert. You're a gem." Bert just smiled and went back into the house. Even though Bert was a man of few words, Mrs. Jenkins usually made up for it by talking twice as much.

In a more serious tone, Mrs. Jenkins said, "Darlin', I don't know what he's done, but all men mess up oncet in a while; heck, us women do too. But I do know one thing; yer John, he's a good man. Take it one day at a time, and don't go flyin' off like some crazy loon who ain't got the good sense God gave a goose."

Before I thought about it, I blurted out, "But he cheated on me...and with my best friend!" Mrs. Jenkins didn't say anything, but put her hand on top of mine. I knew Mrs. Jenkins loved John. He often did electrical work for her and Bert at no charge. He wouldn't take money from them, but he always came home with lots of goodies. Her lemon pound cake was out of this world and her homemade biscuits would melt in your mouth.

"I'm sorry, darlin'. Hey, did I ever tell you the time I cheated on Bert?" I rolled my eyes at her, letting her know that I wasn't that gullible. "It's true! Ask Bert! If he can forgive me, then you can forgive John. All I knowed is that there's two sides to every story, and I can tell you that for free."

"I love you, Mrs. Jenkins. Do you know that you're the highlight of my day?"

"Now that's a shame, and bless yer heart." Squeezing my hand, she said, "I sure look forward to seeing you, Josie girl. Don't get many visitors out this far. Made some pound cake this morning. Ya want some?"

Shaking my head, I said, "I think I'll pass today. Thanks for the tea and the talk."

"You sure you don't want my stick?"

I smiled and said, "Yes, I'm sure. I'll see you tomorrow."

"Remember what I said Josie: one day at a time."

"Yes, ma'am."

John was sitting in one of the chairs on the side porch of the farmhouse when I got home from work. He looked tired. I had only seen him look this miserable one other time in the 26 years we had been married, when his grandmother had just died. They were very close and John took her death very hard.

Taking a deep breath, I walked with dread towards the house. As I got closer to the kitchen door, John stood up and walked towards me. "We can't keep putting this off, Josie. We need to talk." Before I came to the farmhouse, John had slept on the couch while I tried to recuperate from my migraine. I had refused to talk to him because I couldn't look at him without thinking of him and Shelly together.

Something inside me snapped. "I guess we do. Maybe if we had talked a long time ago you wouldn't be screwin' around with my *former* best friend!"

John closed his eyes and took a deep breath. "I'm sorry, Josie."

"Sorry? *Sorry?* Yeah, you're real sorry. You sleep with my best friend and try and blame it on me? I can't bear to look at you! I know I haven't been myself lately, but that is the lowest you could have ever gone. I was grieving for my mama, John, and instead of giving me time, you go to Shelly. Are you so sex deprived that you can't wait for your wife to stop grieving? What is *wrong* with you?" I willed myself not to cry.

"Stop, Josie. I know I have no excuse, but it wasn't like that."

"So what was it like? Was she good in bed? Did she do things I wouldn't do? Did you like her big ol' boobs? Did they turn you on?" I knew I sounded crass, but I was beyond caring anymore.

"Josie, please. Don't. I... I'm sorry, and I don't know what else to say. I know it's not enough, but it's all I have. Please come home."

I couldn't believe he would actually think I would come home. He had made it impossible for me to come home. "John, it's over. I don't hate you, but I can never forgive you. And I can never stop picturing you with Shelly." I looked down and closed my eyes. "You hurt me more than I could ever have imagined. What we had is gone, and we can never get it back." Taking a deep breath, I raised my head and looked into his eyes, seeing pain that matched my own. I hadn't known until that moment what I was going to say. Was it really over?

"I made a huge mistake, Josie. I didn't even realize how much I still loved you until I saw the hurt in your eyes. Can't we try and start over? I promise it will be different." The pleading look in his eyes only made me more determined.

I shook my head. "It's too late. You already made your choice." Without looking back, I walked into the house and quietly shut the door. Feeling numb, I got a glass of water in the kitchen and took four ibuprofen out of the kitchen cabinet. I thought of the miserable look on his face and was actually glad. I hoped his pain was worse than mine. He was the one who messed up. *How can he expect me to just forgive and forget? He made a promise to me almost 26 years ago, and he broke it. The* day of our wedding had been absolutely perfect, and I would never in a million years have thought it would end like this. I guess I was wrong.

Chapter 12

The day had finally arrived. By four o'clock, I would be walking down the aisle and towards the man I was crazy in love with. I couldn't believe it was finally here. Even though I was barely 20, I knew I was old enough to know that being with John for the rest of my life was my destiny. Besides, we just couldn't wait any longer.

John had decided to get his electrician's license and began working as an apprentice for one of his father's friends. Once I graduated high school, I got a job at the local post office. Since I was working full time, I decided to put off going to college. I was making good money and was able to save a nice amount to help us when we began our new life together. We had picked out a nice apartment together, and John had already moved in the month before the wedding.

We planned a small ceremony at my church on the first Saturday in June. Shelly was my maid of honor. The whole day was a blur. I remember floating down the aisle towards John in my secondhand wedding dress, compliments of my cousin Allison. Shelly said my bouquet of fresh daisies were shaking uncontrollably, but I couldn't remember hardly any of it. I do remember kissing John. Preacher Godsey had to clear his throat, indicating our smooch was too long and causing a few chuckles in the church.

After a small reception in the fellowship hall, we headed for Damascus, a small town in Virginia that wasn't too far from our farm. We had rented a small cabin on the river and had great plans of hiking the Appalachian Trail and renting bikes to ride.

The cabin was small, but perfect. Our arms loaded down with luggage, we walked in and set them down in the living room. The sweet smell of pine walls was so inviting, and the stone fireplace looked so quaint. "I love it! This is absolutely wonderful!" I put my bag down and walked to the kitchen to inspect the beautiful daisies, mixed with eucalyptus and baby's breath in a vase on the counter. "Who are these from?"

John walked in behind me and with a smug smile said, "Look at the card."

I grinned back and took the card from the bouquet, reading it out loud. "To the prettiest bride that I get to spend the rest of my life with, beginning tonight. I love you, John." Feeling shy all of a sudden, my face turned red. "Oh, John, they're beautiful. Thank you." The butterflies in my stomach did a few flips. "I love you too."

I couldn't help but feel a little nervous. We were both virgins. I both dreaded and looked forward to the night ahead. I knew John was more than ready. At least we would learn together.

John took my hand and pulled me gently towards him staring intently into my eyes. "I've waited for this night for so long, Josie." He must have seen the trepidation in my eyes. "Are you scared?"

I laid my forehead on his chest and nodded. "A little." I was a lot scared, but I tried to keep this little tidbit to myself. *This is John*, I kept telling myself. *John would never hurt me; well, he wouldn't hurt me intentionally, anyway.* I took a deep breath and slowly looked up. "Are you hungry?" When John just kept looking at me, I stuttered, "W-we can go eat at that little restaurant in town. I've heard they have great hamburgers. I don't know about you, but I'm starving. I couldn't eat a bite this morning, or anything after the wedding. Everything looked so good but...but...John?" I knew I was rambling on and on, but I couldn't help myself. "Can we go and get something to eat?"

John closed his eyes. "Josie, it's okay. You're all nervous, and the more we wait the more nervous you're going to get." John pulled me towards the living room and we sat down on the couch.

Nervously I began looking around the room and noticing little decor touches. "Oh look. I just love the magnolia wreath on the fireplace." John was silent. I took a deep breath and said, "John, I'm sorry. I know it's your first time too. I love you so much and I just want everything to be perfect." I waited for John to respond. Instead of looking at me and reassuring me, he looked down. I saw the faintest hint of pink creeping up his neck. I patted his hand, saying, "It's okay, I'll be fine. We'll be fine." I knew it was time to put my big girl panties on and stop acting like a ninny. I stood up in determination and pulled John's hand.

"Where's the bedroom? Let's go." John was more than glad to show me.

Chapter 13

I woke up Saturday morning and decided it was time to confront Shelly. I knew she would be working at her beauty shop, since Saturday was a busy day for hair. I took a shower and put makeup on for a change. I looked in my suitcase for something to wear and realized I really needed to buy some new clothes. Everything I had was blah, comfy but blah. I put on some jeans and a plain white t-shirt. I tried to fix my hair, thinking it was a shame I couldn't ask Shelly for a trim. Deciding it was hopeless, I put it in a ponytail and headed out the door before I chickened out. All the way there I tried to figure out what I would say to Shelly.

My stomach was in knots because confrontation was something I usually avoided at all costs. Dr. Phil's catchphrase, "How's that working for ya?" kept popping in my head, so I decided I would try to be more assertive from now on. I was tired of people running all over me, and I had to take a stand if I was going to survive. Of course I had to pray for strength too, because my stomach felt as if it would empty itself at any moment. The image of John and Shelly together popped into my head at the strangest moments, and I would catch myself grinding my teeth. Antacid medicines had become my best friend.

The parking lot was full, but that didn't deter me. I was so aggravated I didn't care if the whole town knew what a sorry excuse for a friend Shelly was. Taking a deep breath, I opened my car door and walked with purpose towards Shelly's Hair Hut. I noticed Jenny, Shelly's long-time receptionist, right away; she lowered her head, trying to ignore me. Obviously, she knew Shelly's dirty little secret. I knew Shelly and Jenny were very close and knowing Shelly as I did, she would've had to tell someone about John, so it made sense that it was Jenny. Of course, I knew a couple of Jenny's deep dark secrets, too. Shelly loved to gossip.

Shelly's shop was located on a side street close to downtown. I remembered when Shelly showed it to me the first time, we were both so excited. It was an old two-bedroom house with the cutest front porch. John helped her with the remodel, updating all the electrical work. I helped decorate and even painted women's hair images throughout the main room. Everything was in lavender and black. I couldn't count the number of times my family had sat in those chairs getting their hair cut. I remembered one time I asked Shelly to cut my hair short on a whim. I looked at myself in the big mirror afterwards and began crying uncontrollably. Shelly kept trying to console me, saying John would love it. I knew he wouldn't love it because he had always loved my hair long. John was surprised when he saw me, but told me I always looked beautiful and he would love me no matter what my hair looked like. The boys were a different matter; Tyler cried, and Matt said he liked it better the other way.

The bell jingled as I shut the door of the shop. I walked to the middle of the room and stood there with a disgusted look until I had almost everyone's attention. Several ladies perked up, their faces anticipating their first dose of drama for the day. Myrtle Owens, one of Shelly's regulars, was sitting in a chair with her hair in rollers under the dryer. Her eyes popped open in anticipation. I had been there enough to know that most women came in to talk and gossip as well as get their hair done. *Well, they're gonna get a big dose of drama today!*

Shelly was talking animatedly as she dried a young girl's hair but finally realized there was an abnormal silence in the salon. When she looked up, the color drained from her face and she turned off the blow dryer. We stared at each other for a few seconds until Shelly whispered something in the girl's ear. Placing the dryer and brush on the counter, she walked towards me with something like trepidation in her eyes. She said, "I wasn't expecting you, Josie."

Talking through gritted teeth, I hissed, "I just bet you weren't." A young girl working one of the chairs beside Shelly clapped her hand to her face and a little squeak came out of her mouth.

Closing her eyes, Shelly looked apprehensive but mostly resigned to the inevitable. "Why don't we go in the back room where we can talk privately?" Shelly had one of the bedrooms set up as a lounge. There was a sofa bed and two comfy chairs, along with a television so she could keep up with her soaps. We spent a lot of time in that room together. Our kids would play video games or watch television while we talked. She looked at me with pleading eyes, begging me not to cause a scene. I shook my head. With the mood I was in, it just wasn't possible.

I followed Shelly into the room and once I was in, she quietly shut the door and leaned against it. I pointed at her with my stubby, chewed up fingernail and said with as much menace as I could, "I just wanted you to know...you have got some nerve. If you call yourself a friend, I sure would hate to see my enemies. You better *never* go near John again. Do you hear me? If you do, you'll be sorry! I'll never, *ever*, forgive you as long as I live!"

Shelly stared back but instead of being remorseful, she looked annoyed. "Could you please lower your voice, Josie? This is not the time or place for this."

"Really? What, you think we should go have a cup of coffee and talk? Are you kidding me?" I was incensed. What kind of person steals her best friend's husband and doesn't show any shame whatsoever? Did I know her at all? I knew that Shelly could be unscrupulous, but to her best friend?

Shelly took a deep breath and actually had the audacity to talk to me as if I was a child. "You need to calm down. I don't know what you're talking about and if we can't discuss this in a civilized manner, you need to leave this shop."

"Shelly!" I had to try and get some kind of sense out of this whole morbid situation. Two important people in my world had just betrayed me, horribly. "Shelly, how could you? How could you do this to me? I've loved you since we were kids!"

Finally, I detected a slight look of remorse in her eyes. I knew my Shelly inside and out. I knew the good and I knew the bad, but this Shelly was someone I didn't know at all. As if shaking herself, Shelly opened door. "I think you need to leave."

Knowing it was useless to try and make sense of anything I nodded. "I'll leave Shelly, but don't ever call me or come near me or my family ever again. You got it?" Shelly's face was like a mask. There was no feeling, no expression, just...nothing.

As I walked out, I couldn't help but notice how everyone's mouths were hanging open. The silence was so palpable you could hear a pin drop. Realizing confronting Shelly was a complete waste of time, I walked out of Shelly's shop with my head held high. I can't believe I thought it would do any good to confront her. I still felt some sort of satisfaction; I was proud for actually standing up for myself. Confronting John and Shelly was over.

I walked to my car and got in, buckling my seat belt. *It's done*, I told myself. Things could get back to normal now. I could start over, and things would get better. They had to get better. I could live without John, and I could live without Shelly. I could be happy again. I might even find someone else to love, eventually.

I smiled and then giggled, thinking I would love to be a fly on the wall in Shelly's shop. I could just imagine everyone's big eyes looking at Shelly, wondering what was going on. My giggles eventually turned into sobs.

Chapter 14

Two people couldn't have been more in love than John and I. The first year of our marriage was like a fairytale. We didn't have much money, but that didn't seem to bother us. We had so much more. We went through our days with starry eyes and our nights with complete and total bliss. We didn't get much sleep, but we were young and didn't need it. Being so happy and content transferred to my artwork. John was my favorite subject, especially when he was doing something on the farm, like fishing or riding one of the tractors. I never tired of bringing him to life because each stroke of my brush was made with an adoring love.

Shelly would often complain that we never spent much time together anymore. I felt bad but knew that once she was married, she would understand. She went from boyfriend to boyfriend, trying to find someone as wonderful as John. It was impossible.

In frustration, Shelly said, "I just wish I could find someone who looks at me the way that John looks at you."

I couldn't help but smile. I knew I was lucky because when John looked at me with those incredible green eyes, my insides would melt. When we were alone, he couldn't keep his hands off of me. I loved knowing he wanted me every second of every day just by the look of raw hunger in his eyes.

"You'll find him Shelly, and then you'll be as happy as me." I hoped it would be soon, so she would quit whining about it. Every man she ever dated, she quickly found fault with. He wasn't cute enough, wasn't considerate enough, didn't have enough ambition, or didn't make enough money. If she stayed with someone more than a couple of months, it was a big surprise.

Eventually, she did meet someone she liked enough to marry. His name was Allen, and he was a few years older than Shelly. He sold insurance, had been married once before, and had a teenage son. They married quickly. Shelly was tired of the dating scene, and Allen didn't have a chance once Shelly made up her mind. The marriage didn't turn out to be perfect, though, and they were divorced a year later. I never saw two people who hated each other as much as they did afterward. Shelly told me it was the biggest mistake she ever made. She thought he had money, but he was actually in a lot of debt. Any extra money he had went to his ex-wife in alimony plus child support. According to Shelly, he was also lazy, spineless, and had terrible morning breath. She was never going to get married again unless she knew it would be forever.

When I found out I was pregnant with our first child, I was surprised but happy. We wanted to wait, but God had other plans for us. Matthew was the sweetest baby, and made our little family perfect. John was so proud of his son and worked even harder to make sure that we had everything we needed. I continued working at the post office, and we saved every extra dime for our future.

Shelly soon met Jared and fell head over heels in love. Forgetting her vow to wait, they married soon after. Jared swept Shelly off her feet, and their marriage began as a happy one. We found out that we were both pregnant at the same time and Tyler and Carly were born a month apart, Tyler being the oldest.

Because we were running out of room in our small apartment, John and I decided to rent a small two-bedroom house and continue saving our money so we could eventually build our dream home. My parents gave us five acres for it, and we knew just the spot where we wanted to build.

Shelly's husband made good money working as a contractor, and they built a brand-new house in a new development in town. For a while, Shelly was ecstatic in her marriage and proud of her new home. But after Carly was born, things weren't so perfect anymore. Shelly complained constantly that Jared worked long hours and left her home alone all day with the baby. I wanted to tell her to get over it because he was only trying to make a living, and she wouldn't like it if he was poor and stayed home. She was also fortunate because she didn't have to work. I was thankful that my mother helped take care of our boys while I worked, but I would have loved to stay at home and take care of them myself.

Watching Shelly's marriage slowly fall apart again made me even more thankful for John. John worked hard, but he also made time for the boys and me. Our days were hectic and I cherished every moment our family was together. John began helping my father more and more at the farm. The boys and I would often spend our evenings with my mom while John and my father took care of the never-ending chores. The boys loved their mamaw just as much as she loved them. Through this time, we grew even closer. I worried that she wasn't happy; I could see the sadness in her eyes. The boys made her smile, and she loved to spoil them rotten. She told me more than once to be thankful for what John and I shared because it was special, and not everyone was so lucky.

I knew my dad wasn't the easiest person to live with. He always seemed to be grouchy or tired. I knew there wasn't any hope for us to have a great relationship, but I had hoped that it would be better with Matt and Tyler. Mom often made excuses for him and tried to make up for it by loving them twice as much, just as she did me. John's father was the papaw they loved best because he took them fishing a lot. He would also get in the floor and wrestle with them, or play with their toys.

Mom and I had been working every weekend on an upstairs bedroom for weeks. Mom had decided the boys needed a playroom, and begged me to do a mural in one of the extra bedrooms. I hadn't been painting much since the boys were born but thought it might be fun. Every wall focused on their favorite Disney characters, and they loved it. One whole wall was devoted to their favorite Disney movie, *The Jungle Book*. Mom had tears in her eyes when it was finally finished. "I'm so proud of you, sweetheart. You're so talented."

I smiled and said, "Thank you, Mama. I'm glad you talked me into it. I've really enjoyed painting again."

"You just amaze me. I don't have an artistic bone in my body."

I laughed because I knew it was true. Even Dad couldn't draw a straight line. "Usually, being artistic runs in the family. We must have some relatives somewhere down the line that had some creative ability. Wonder who they were?" I was confused when Mama looked down, as if embarrassed about something. She looked at me so intently that I said, "What?"

She opened her mouth but no words came out. Then she changed the subject. "I bet the boys are hungry. Let's go eat. Who wants spaghetti?" Matt and Tyler both jumped up at the same time and shouted, "Me!" As we all walked downstairs, I wondered what she had been about to say.

Chapter 15

Before paramedics came and carted me off to some mental hospital, I made myself stop crying. I had to be strong. Falling apart was not an option. Beginning now was the rest of my life, and I knew it must be with resilience. The fog had vanished and the light was bright. Boy was it bright.

I started the engine and turned the heat wide open. I was shivering as if it was 30 degrees outside instead of a balmy 80. Somehow, I drove from Shelly's to the grocery store without mishap. Taking a deep breath and wiping the tears from my face, I climbed out of the car and took out the list Mary had given me that morning.

Strolling down the dairy isle with my head down and hoping I wouldn't see anyone I knew, I accidentally bumped into another cart. "Oh! Excuse me." I looked up and saw Kyle Richardson, a friend of John's. Kyle installed air conditioner and heating units. He had worked with John on several projects.

"Well, hey, Josie! How are ya?" Kyle had moved back to our area about five years ago from Charlotte, North Carolina. He and his wife had divorced, so he moved to be near his elderly parents. His children were all grown up and on their own.

"I'm fine, Kyle. You?" I tried to smile. John thought a lot of Kyle. He always talked about how nice he was and how honest.

"Pretty good. Mom wanted me to pick up a few things for her. Hey, can you have John call me? I have a side job for him and I think he'll be real interested."

"Well...um...I guess you'll need to call him yourself. We've...actually, we've separated." I had to take a deep breath, forcing myself not to cry.

"Man, I'm so sorry Josie." Kyle started shaking his head as if in shock. "I know it's tough. Been there, done that."

I nodded, afraid that if I spoke my voice would betray me. Kyle said, "Look, if there's anything I can do, just let me know. Sometimes it helps just to have someone to talk to."

"Thank you, Kyle. I appreciate it."

"Okay...well, I guess I better get mom's toilet plunger." As he rolled his eyes, he held up a piece of paper. "That's number one on her list." I couldn't help but giggle. "I'm serious; call if you need a friend."

I smiled as he walked away, thinking, *Well, that wasn't so bad. One down and a few hundred to go.* I also thought about how nice Kyle was and decided maybe, just maybe, I would take him up on his offer.

Mary was sitting in the living room with Dad when I got home. After I put the groceries away, I sat down next to her on the couch. She put down the book she had been reading and asked, "Are you okay?"

"Let's just say it's been an interesting morning. How's Dad?" The vacant look in his eyes told me things hadn't changed much. Being around him more in these past few days had been harder than I thought. Seeing your father deteriorate in mind and body was extremely difficult.

"The same. I have some good news, though. The facility I told you about has an opening soon. He could have a room sooner than we thought."

"That's great, Mary. I can't imagine how hard it's been for you. I know I don't tell you enough how much I appreciate you." I hadn't realized before how hard it was for Mary. Even though we had a home health care nurse for the day, Mary usually had no help through the nights. Some nights were fine; other nights seemed never ending, when he couldn't seem to sleep or rest.

Mary shrugged. "What else am I going to do? By the way, John came by this morning." Mary looked back at her book and didn't offer any further information.

"He did? What did he want?" I wondered if he found out about what I did at Shelly's shop. My face turned red when I thought about how out of character it was for me to make a scene like that.

As if she was embarrassed, Mary said, "He wanted to apologize for... for what he did to you. He's worried about you."

"Does he just expect me to forgive him and pretend it never happened? I can't do that, Mary. He did something unforgivable, having an affair with Shelly!" I pulled my knees up and hugged them.

"I know. You have to do what you have to do. I just wanted you to know what he said."

"Yeah, well, thanks." I started rubbing my temples, feeling the throbbing begin once again. "I think I'll do some cleaning to help get my mind off of everything. Do you need me to do anything else?"

"If you can watch Dad for a while this evening, I would appreciate it. I need to run some errands." I knew it was more than errands but as usual, Mary would tell me in her own sweet time, and not a minute before.

I decided I'd better take some ibuprofen first, just in case. Then I went upstairs to begin cleaning Dad's room since he was downstairs. I opened the windows to let in some fresh air. The room had an odor, which wasn't uncommon for someone like Dad, who had lost all ability to control his functions. Once it was clean and smelled fresher, I walked into the boy's old playroom. I couldn't help but smile, thinking back to the special times I spent with Mom decorating this room. I would give anything to be able to go back to those days when everything was perfect, when John loved me and kept his promises, and my mom was always there to hold me and tell me everything would be all right.

The room wasn't messy, just a little dusty. It had been a long time since the boys played there. The race car track took up almost half of the room. In no time, I cleaned the furniture and mopped the floors. Maybe I would have grandchildren one day and they would enjoy this room like their daddies had. Knowing John and I wouldn't enjoy our grandchildren together brought fresh tears to my eyes. Before I turned off the light, I noticed that the red wagon was broken. I couldn't bear to throw it out, so instead I took it up to the attic. My first thought was that maybe John could fix it later. I would have to stop thinking like that.

It wasn't easy, but I finally got the attic stairs down and carried the wagon up the steps. It had been years since I had been in the attic. Thankfully, the light still worked but it showed me that everything was covered with a fine layer of dust. Walking around, I looked at old furniture, tons of cardboard boxes, and lots of broken items, like old sewing machines and clocks. It would take months to go through all of this stuff. I wondered if Mary ever came up here. I could see that there were footprints in the dust, so she must have been up here at some point. They led to a group of boxes in one corner. I looked to see what they were and found *important papers* written on one of the boxes.

As I opened the box, I sneezed when the dust began floating up to my nose. It looked like it was nothing but insurance policies and Dad's army papers. I was about to close it when I noticed an envelope marked *birth certificates*. I got excited because I had never seen my birth certificate. I opened the folder and saw that mine was on top. Scanning through the document I checked all of the information: *Josie Marie Taylor, six pounds and five ounces, January 15, 1968, mother: Sarah Jane Taylor, father: David M. Murray.* I read it again, thinking there must be a mistake—but there it was, in black and white. Who the heck was David M. Murray, and why was he listed as my father?

I took the document and sat down on a dusty chair in the middle of the room. My mind was going in a million different directions. How could this be? Why didn't my mother tell me? Did I know David M. Murray? With all the questions I had, one thing became clear; I finally knew why I never felt a connection with my father. He had known, and he didn't love me because of it. Everything suddenly fell into place. Realizing it was getting late, I dusted my behind and anywhere else I could see dust. I carefully walked down the steps and closed the attic door.

In a daze, I went downstairs and sat on the couch in the living room. Looking at the man I had thought for 46 years was my father, I couldn't help but be sad. Even though he didn't love me like he did Mary, I still loved him. I remember as a child always trying to please him, but never measuring up. It wasn't until I got older that I had realized we would probably never be close. I gave up trying, but I never gave up hope. I always thought that one day he would look at me and we would finally have that father-daughter moment. He would tell me that he was proud of me, and he had always loved me.

Guess that's never going to happen now. Oh, Mama, what did you do? Is it true? Did you have an affair? Were you raped? Is my real father a rapist? My mind was going in so many directions.

I could hear Mary in the kitchen. She walked in with her pocketbook and said, "I'm leaving now. I'll see you tonight."

"Okay." I was still in shock and couldn't think of anything else to say.

Mary looked at me funny. "Are you okay?"

"I'm fine. Have fun." I tried to smile, but I'm sure it came out more as a grimace.

Mary hesitated for just a moment, then shrugged and walked out the door. Dad slowly got out of his chair and started walking in circles around the room. I could tell that it was getting harder for him to get up and down. Since there was no cable this far out in the country, we had a satellite dish. I put the television on the classic country music station, hoping it would soothe him and make him feel more relaxed. I loved it because it always brought me back to when I was young and that was the only music we ever listened to. After a few minutes, he stopped in the middle of the room and stood there until I led him back to his chair. After I fed him some scrambled eggs that Mary had left on the counter, he drifted off to sleep.

Thinking it was probably a waste of time, I got up and found the phone book, looking to see if there were any David M. Murrays listed. My eyes grew big when I saw the name. There was a listing for David M. Murray on the east side of town, near the railroad station. Was he the same David on my birth certificate? This was just crazy!

I sat down in one of the kitchen chairs and thought about calling John to tell him about what I had found, then realized that I couldn't call him. I had no mother, no best friend, and no husband.

I looked through the kitchen and into the living room where my dad was sitting in his chair. Could he really not be my father? Maybe this was all just a big mistake, or a bad dream. *Maybe this whole week was a bad dream and I'll wake up tomorrow back in my old bed, next to John.* I missed my home and even after all that had happened, I missed my husband.

Chapter 16

I'll never forget the day we finally moved into our dream home. Knowing we had worked so hard and saved for so long made it all the more gratifying. John and I had dreamed of building our own log cabin since our honeymoon. John actually picked me up and carried me through the front door while the boys stood there laughing. Matt was nine and Tyler was seven at the time. Once inside, John set me down and pulled me into his arms, kissing me on the mouth. At first it was just a little kiss, but it soon turned more exuberant.

"Gross! We're going to our room!" I heard the boys run by but I was too busy to notice much of anything. John and I kissed our way to our bedroom but before we could shut the door, we heard someone knocking.

"Anybody home? I brought y'all some dinner." My mom stood there holding a casserole dish with her oven mittens. "It's chicken and rice, and it's nice and hot."

I giggled when John groaned in frustration. I ran to my mother and hugged her. "Thanks, Mama! Isn't it great? I still have a lot of stuff to put away, but we're finally going to be able to sleep in our very own home." I started jumping up and down and squealed, "I'm so excited!"

"You deserve it. You've worked hard for it."

"We couldn't have done it without the land, though. Thank you again. It's absolutely perfect." As we walked into the kitchen, I said, "This looks delicious. Are you going to eat with us?"

"No, sweetie. I need to get back. Mary is at the house. I'm not sure, but I think her and Dale are calling it quits. I better get back and see what's going on."

"Oh no, I hope not." I wasn't surprised. They hadn't been married long, but even when they first got married, I told John it just didn't seem right. They didn't act anything like a newly-married couple usually acted. The only time I saw them kiss was the day of their wedding. Mary wasn't the most affectionate person, but sometimes it seemed as if she didn't even like Dale.

That evening after supper, I couldn't wait to sit in our new rockers on the porch. Dragging John outside with me, I made him sit down and relax. "I know you probably have a million things to do, but I want you to just sit and enjoy the moment." It was a beautiful autumn evening and the sun was peeking through the trees just on top of the hill. We had picked this spot so we could enjoy the sunsets every night. Feeling happy, I got out of my chair and sat on John's lap, placing my arms around his neck and my cheek on his chest. "I love you, John."

John pulled me closer and kissed the top of my head. We sat that way until the sun disappeared over the hill and the boys came running outside. "We're going to look for fireflies. Can you get us a jar, Mom?"

"I have no idea what box my jars are in. Sorry, Matt. Why don't you just use a cup?"

"They can't use a cup. Come on boys, I'll find a jar in the barn." After John led the boys to the barn I decided to work on those boxes. I got tired after emptying a couple so I decided to take a bubble bath in our new garden bathtub. It was like heaven, sinking down into those bubbles. I was almost asleep when I heard them all come back in.

John walked in and leaned against the doorframe. He looked at me a few minutes and then said, "I'll put the boys to bed. Be back soon."

I smiled because I knew that look. Getting out of the tub, I put some scented lotion on and then got in the bed naked. I pulled the covers up so that they just covered me and waited. The longer I waited, the heavier my eyelids became and soon I was sound asleep.

The weight of John pressing down on the bed caused my eyes to flutter open. "Sorry it took so long. The boys and I got into a long discussion about dinosaurs and which ones were the best."

"That's okay. I was just resting my eyes." I felt the blanket being pulled down slowly. The cool air raised goose pimples on my skin.

My hands automatically moved to cover myself but John took both hands and raised them above my head. He whispered "Don't." I watched him look down at my body. After having two children it wasn't like it used to be. My cesarean scar stood out and I had put on a few extra pounds. I was still self-conscious.

I struggled with humiliation and closed my eyes. "Please, John. Don't look that close. It's embarrassing."

"Open your eyes, Josie." I opened them slowly. John leaned down and kissed me on the lips, then looked in my eyes. "You are still the most beautiful woman in the world to me." His lips trailed to my neck. "I love every freckle and every scar. I love every inch of you, and you'll always be perfect to me."

I smiled lazily and licked my lips. "I love you, too."

Chapter 17

A couple of weeks later I was drinking a cup of coffee in the kitchen on a Sunday morning, listening to the radio. I still refused to talk to John. I had dressed for church, but I kept making excuses for not going. First of all, I cringed when I thought of how I acted the last time I was in church. Second, news spread fast in our little town. I knew I was being a coward, but I just couldn't face the look of pity on everyone's faces. I could just imagine Mrs. Riddle giving me one of her condescending looks. *See what happens when you try and sit in someone else's pew?* Mary hardly ever went to church anymore, even when I offered to sit with Dad.

Taking my coffee into the living room, I sat beside Mary. She was working a crossword puzzle from the newspaper, one of her favorite pastimes. I noticed that she had a few more gray hairs around her temple. She had cut her beautiful curls a long time ago and now wore it layered and short. She never wore makeup, but she really didn't need any. Her skin had always been clear and smooth.

Dad was dozing in his chair. I still couldn't believe he wasn't my real father but his distance towards my children and me all made sense now. He probably couldn't look at me without thinking that I had ruined his life somehow; like I did it on purpose. I wanted to talk to Mary about it, but something held me back. Would she feel the same way as my father? Our relationship wasn't the best now; would this make it worse? I didn't want to take that chance. I thought of the footprints in the attic. Maybe she already knew.

"I'm going to head out now. I'll see you in a little bit." Mary barely looked up. I rinsed my cup, placed it in the sink and then grabbed my pocketbook. It was already hot outside, so I turned the air conditioner on in the car and pulled out of the driveway. Instead of going to church, I headed in the opposite direction, toward town. I turned on the radio and tried not to think of where I was actually going. As I eventually turned on to the street I had memorized in my head, my heart began racing. *What am I doing?* I thought. *No good can come of this...it's probably a waste of time.* I couldn't stop myself though, and drove until I found the address I was looking for. After pulling over next to the curb, I put my head down in my hands and prayed that God would give me guidance and strength. After a few moments I felt a little better, a little calmer.

Taking a deep breath, I looked up and studied the house. It was a nice, brick ranch with a huge oak tree in the front yard. It looked like every other house in the neighborhood. Was this where my real father lived? A black pickup was sitting in the carport, so someone must be home. I had come this far, but I knew I didn't have enough nerve to walk to the door, ring the bell, and say, "Hello, I think I'm your daughter." It was definitely too soon for that. I was still trying to adjust to the fact that Dad wasn't my real dad. The whole situation was too bizarre. As if everything I had been through with John and Shelly wasn't enough, then I find out my real dad is a complete and total stranger.

My cell phone began vibrating, causing me to jump. I looked down and saw John's name on my caller I.D. I almost didn't answer, but changed my mind at the last minute. "Hello."

"Josie, Matt called. He and Tyler are coming over. They said they would be here a little after noon." I groaned out loud because I wasn't ready for this. Not even close. "We need to talk before they get here. Can you come over?"

It was the last thing I wanted to do at that moment but I said, "Okay. I'll be there soon." I started the engine and put the car in gear. Before I drove off, I saw a man that looked to be in his seventies walk from the front door towards the truck wearing a suit. He was looking towards my car with curiosity. I was frozen in fear. The man stopped and stared. Scared out of my wits, I took off, not looking back. Why did I feel as if I was doing something wrong? Anyone would have some curiosity about someone they just found out was their father. Taking another deep breath, I headed to the farm. I didn't want to face John, but knew it was unavoidable.

He was sitting on the front porch in a rocker as I pulled up. The first thing I noticed was the dark circles under his eyes. He had a t-shirt and jeans on, and it looked like he hadn't shaved in a couple of days. Even after all these years, I still thought of him as the most handsome man I knew. Working on the farm kept him in good shape, and it showed. I thought of my own body, going soft with neglect. Getting out of the car, I slowly walked up to the porch with dread. I could get on with my life easier if I didn't have to deal with seeing John like this. Having children together made that impossible.

Scooting to the edge of his seat, John said, "Did you go to church?"

I shook my head. "I was going to, but decided to go for a drive instead."

"You look good, Josie. I miss you."

"Don't do this, John. It's hard enough." I sat down and refused to look at him. As I rubbed my temples, I asked, "What are we going to tell the boys?'

After a few seconds, John said, "Let's just not say anything right now. Can't we pretend, just for today, that nothing's changed?"

I finally looked closely and saw the tears in John's eyes. For a moment, I almost felt sorry for him. I knew it was a mistake, that we needed to get it over with, but I dreaded it as much as he did. I didn't want to see the hurt in my children's eyes when they found out their parents were getting a divorce. Against my better judgment, I nodded and said, "Okay, but we need to tell them soon. We can't keep putting this off."

I could see the relief in John's eyes and wished things were different. Why did he have to ruin everything? In a harsher voice than I intended, I said, "We need to figure out what we're going to do. We'll need a lawyer."

"Josie, please, don't do this. I'll do anything to make it up to you. I was wrong and I made a horrible mistake."

In exasperation, I shouted, "John, you can't do enough to make it up to me! Don't you understand?" With my voice dripping in disgust, I said, "Tell me something; did you think of me at all while you were in her arms?" I couldn't stop the tears flowing down my face. "Did our marriage vows mean nothing to you?" In exasperation, I jumped out of my chair and ran into the house. Before I could make it to the bedroom and shut the door, John was there and stopped it with his foot. He pushed it open until it slammed against the wall. I backed up into the room until my legs were against the bed. We were both furious and breathing heavily.

Taking my arms, he pulled me against his chest. I pushed and struggled with all my strength but knew it was pointless. With his chin against the top of my head, John cried, "It meant nothing to me, Josie! I regretted it as soon as it happened. That night when I was talking to Shelly on the phone, I told her it was a mistake, that it never should have happened."

I went still and stopped struggling; my face in his chest. "Give me a break. You were making plans to go to her house! Were you going to tell her before or after you had sex again?"

"I was going to end it!"

"Well, maybe she'll take you back now that we're through."

"We'll never be through, Josie." I pushed him again and John finally relented. He stepped back but put his hands on my shoulders. His eyes were intense but unerringly clear. "I know you're hurting right now. I deserve everything you're throwing at me and more, but I still love you. If I have to prove to you every day how much I love you, I will. No matter what it takes."

Before I could say anything, we heard the boys holler as they came through the front door. "Wash up. I'll talk to them until you come out." John kissed the top of my head and then went out the bedroom door. I wanted to scream in frustration.

After a few moments I put a smile on my face and walked into the living room. "Hey, boys!"

"Hey, Mom! Have you guys had lunch?" Matt was looking at me with a sweet smile on his face. I should have known they would be hungry. Usually I would have made a big lunch because Sunday was one of the only days they visited, and they always wanted a home-cooked meal.

"I don't have any lunch prepared; I've been spending a lot of time helping Mary with your grandfather. Would a sandwich be okay?"

I could tell they were both disappointed until John said, "Let's just go out and get something and give your mom a break."

Both boys jumped up and Tyler said, "Cool. Let's go, I'm starved! Can we go to Burger Bar?"

John picked up his truck keys from the counter. "Sounds good to me."

I hesitated, then decided to go along. Maybe this would be the last time we would all be together. I hoped I could keep it together. As we drove to the restaurant, I tried not to look at John because every time I did, I wished for something that could never be again. Tyler was chattering in the back seat about his new summer job. He was working at a local department store in their security department. "You wouldn't believe how many people steal stuff. This one old lady had her pocketbook full of crap and acted like we were the criminals when we asked her to empty her purse."

Matt just laughed and said, "People are crazy. I'm amazed every day and think it can't get worse, but it does." I couldn't help but worry about Matt. Being a police officer was so dangerous. If something ever happened to him or Tyler, I would never recover. Matt and Tyler were both built like their father and had his green eyes. Matt had John's dark hair, and Tyler had my blonde hair. They were both so handsome, and always had girls chasing after them. As far as I knew, neither one had a serious girlfriend at the moment.

"Matt, please be careful. I don't know what I would do if something happened to you." I wished I hadn't sounded so pathetic. The boys hated it when I worried.

Sounding very serious, Matt said, "I will, Mom. Just the other day I was in a situation: This old lady called nine-one-one, and when I got there, I had to break down the door. Just when I thought things were hopeless, I heard a faint cry coming from the bathroom. I ran down the hall, opened the door, and she was trying to open her medicine bottle. It was so sad. Poor thing was about to give up."

Tyler was laughing, and John was grinning. "You! That isn't funny, and you shouldn't tease your mother." I tried to keep from smiling but failed miserably. "One of these days, you might not be able to open your medicine bottle and then you'll be sorry for making fun of old ladies."

"I'm just sayin' that I deal with stuff like that way more often than with anything remotely serious. You have nothing to be worried about. I'm the rookie; they always give me the lame calls." Matt shrugged his shoulders, "So don't worry, you're just wasting your time."

"I'm your mother. It's my job to worry about you."

"You're really going to worry when we're both police officers, then." Tyler had his eyebrows raised and an apologetic look on his face.

"Oh, great. I'll never get a good night's rest again." I started shaking my head. I knew it was coming, but still hoped he would change his mind.

John said, "So you've made up your mind, then? Do you want to stay in Johnson City with your brother?"

"Maybe. I guess I'll go wherever I can find a job."

We pulled into the parking lot and took one of the last parking spaces. We waited a few minutes at the restaurant door, but were finally seated. As we all sat down at the table, I looked at John. I turned quickly away because I couldn't stand the pleading look in his eyes. It broke my heart to know that this family would never be the same, but it wasn't my fault; I wasn't the one who had broken my vows. What if I was the one who had the affair? Would John be so quick to forgive me? I didn't think so. What would he think if he knew I had thought about calling Kyle Richardson? I did think about it, but couldn't quite bring myself to do it. Instead, I would try and enjoy this last time together as a family. I wasn't a good actress, but I would do my best to fake it. Hopefully I could control the fist that still wanted to punch John in the face.

Chapter 18

As we settled into our new home, life became busier than ever. Matt and Tyler loved sports and were involved in something every season. If I wasn't working, I was running the boys back and forth to games or practice. John helped as much as he could, but with his job and trying to keep up with everything on the farm, he barely had time to turn around himself. My dad came to depend on him more and more. He was quite a few years older than Mom, and he was beginning to show his age.

The only time John and I had alone anymore was when we went to bed. Usually we were both so tired that we were asleep as soon as our heads hit the pillows. I missed the nights when John and I couldn't keep our hands off of each other, but not enough to lose precious sleep.

I had been given my own route at work, which was wonderful. I enjoyed being by myself all day with nothing to worry about but getting the right mail in the right box. I had a new reason to save now; every extra dime now went in the bank for the boys' college education.

I began smoking at work. Everyone at the post office smoked and soon I did too, just to be able to take a regular break. At first, I would just stand outside pretending, but soon I began inhaling and puffing just like everyone else. I knew it was stupid, but I couldn't help myself. I was smoking during my routes just to relieve the boredom, but I never smoked at home or around my family. Gradually I came to depend on the cigarettes more and more, and would even wake up at night craving them. Sometimes I would make an excuse to leave the house just so I could smoke.

One day I was on my route, smoking like a freight train, when I passed my mother. She slowed down and looked at me with her mouth hanging wide open. I was so embarrassed and my face turned blood red. That night she came over and asked me to take a short walk with her. "I've got to start dinner, Mama. John will be here soon, and..."

"Young lady, you get your butt out here right now." Feeling like a child, I put the pot back on the stove and walked outside.

"I want you to know that when I saw you today, I was shocked. I couldn't believe you were smoking! *Smoking!* Have you lost your mind?" Before I could say anything in my defense, she continued, "Years ago people didn't know any better, but now they do. I thought you were smarter than that, Josie Marie. I have never been more disappointed in you."

Hanging my head, I mumbled, "I'm sorry, Mama."

"I've had my suspicions for a while, but I couldn't believe that you would actually do something so stupid. You have got to quit, Josie. I will not have my daughter dying of lung cancer. I watched my mother die a slow horrible death when she was only sixty-five. Do you know what it's like to gasp for every breath you take? It's horrendous! You've got to quit now, before it's too late!"

"It's not that easy, Mama." I was so ashamed. I couldn't stand to have my mom disappointed in me, but I wasn't sure if I could do it.

"I know it's not easy, but you have to do it. You don't have a choice. Does John know?"

"I don't think so. If he does, he hasn't said anything."

"You can do it Josie, if you set your mind to it. I won't say anything else, but I'll be watching you. I can't help but be disappointed. But you know I love you more than anything, right?" Taking my hand, she brought it to her lips and kissed it.

"Okay, Mama. I love you too." We walked back to the house in silence. Before leaving, she hugged me and then walked back home. I watched her leave and prayed that God would give me the strength to quit. I wanted to quit for her as much as for me. I couldn't stand the smell of smoke on my clothes or on my breath. I brushed my teeth all the time, afraid they would turn yellow and gross. Sometimes I would see someone talking and smoking at the same time, with their cigarette bobbing up and down and think they looked so silly. I knew I didn't want to look like that.

The following day, I thought I would go crazy. By that night I was so grouchy that John said, "Why don't I take the boys out for a hamburger so you can be alone? That is, if you can stand yourself."

"I'm sorry, John! It's just been a bad day." I felt bad for being so crabby, but I couldn't help myself. I was so desperate that I almost asked him to pick up a pack of cigarettes on his way home. Why did I throw them all away? If I had just one, that was all I needed to take the edge off. Then I would be myself again.

"Are you sure that's all it is?" He looked at me funny, as if he knew.

"Yes, John. I've got a bad headache. Maybe if I take a bath and lay down, I'll feel better." I just couldn't tell him the truth. John had used smokeless tobacco sometimes when he was younger, and I had given him a hard time about it. What a hypocrite I was.

"Okay. We'll probably swing by and get some ice cream, too. You want me to bring you something?"

"A strawberry sundae would be nice." I smiled. "Thank you. I'm sorry for being such a grouch."

Taking me in his arms, he kissed me and said, "That's okay. I love you."

"I love you, too." For the first time that day, I actually felt as if I could survive the hell I had put myself through. John could always make me feel better. All it took was a look or a touch, and all my worries would dissipate like the fog on a hot summer morning. Of course, ice cream helped too.

That night, John climbed in bed and pulled me to him. Even though we didn't make love as often, when we did it was still wonderful. I needed him so much, and for a while I didn't think about anything but the way my body responded to his touch.

By the end of the week, I finally felt as if I could make it. Each day was as hard as the last but I knew that there was a light at the end of the tunnel, and it wasn't at the end of a cigarette. I had chewed so much gum that my jaw was sore, but I was finally smoke-free. I didn't have to rush in the house and throw my clothes in the washer before anyone else smelled them, or waste money on a filthy habit.

One early Saturday morning, Shelly and I were standing on the sidelines watching the kids play soccer. Tyler and Carly were on the same team. She knew I had been smoking. Sometimes we would do it together, but she never knew how bad it had gotten. When I told her I had quit, she said, "Why? Sometimes I think that's the only enjoyment I get."

Shelly and Jared were finally getting a divorce. It was a long time coming and I was surprised it lasted as long as it did. "Mom caught me, and I knew it was time to quit anyway. It was getting to the point that I was craving them more and more."

Shelly started laughing and said, "My mom smokes more than me! She could care less if I quit." Shelly's mother had been smoking as long as I had known her. There were always ashtrays full of her lipstick-stained menthol cigarette butts laying around the house. Shelly and I would sneak and smoke her cigarettes sometimes when we were teenagers. I can still see Shelly making fun of her with a cigarette bobbing up and down in her mouth. "Shelly Francis Gibson! Get your lazy ass up and clean that nasty room!" or "You're just like your good for nothin' father," and her favorite, "I brought you into this world, Shelly Francis, and I can take you right back out, too!" Her mom had a terrible smoker's voice now. I couldn't believe she hadn't keeled over from lung cancer yet. The woman survived on Diet Pepsi and cigarettes.

We both laughed. "Well, I'm glad I did it. The only bad thing is I can't quit eating. I'm afraid to get on the scales because I know I've gained weight."

"There's no way I'm quitting! I'm fat enough. If my boobs get any bigger, I'm going to have to start ordering my bras in special sizes." I started giggling. "It's true! I used to be proud, but now they're just a hassle...and my back has been killing me. Besides, when I try to cut some-one's hair, especially a man's, it's really hard to keep these puppies form brushing up against them. Of course, most men don't seem to mind."

"Well, I was going to say something. Every time you cut my hair, I was wondering if you were doing it on purpose." I tried to look serious, but laughed out loud instead.

"I would give anything to be as small as you." After I raised my eye-brows, Shelly said, "I mean...not that you don't have boobs, it's just that you're not...overloaded."

"John doesn't seem to mind, so I guess I'm happy." John always told me he thought my breasts were perfect, not too small and not too big, just right. I knew they weren't perfect; actually, one was just a little bit bigger than the other, but he didn't seem to notice or care.

"You're so lucky, Josie. Maybe next time I'll find my John." I didn't say anything, but I thought even if she did find someone like John, she would still find fault with him. Shelly was the type of girl who could never be satisfied. She liked to flirt outrageously, and being a hairdresser gave her plenty of opportunities. She probably brushed up on a lot of men on purpose.

After the game, I offered to take Carly with me so Shelly could go to work, promising to drop her off later. I had to get home, then I needed to take Matt to his soccer game later that day. Having Carly with us would keep Tyler from getting bored. Carly was already showing signs of being a real beauty, but she was still a tomboy. She would much rather play with the boys and their toys than play with dolls, much to Shelly's disappointment. Gone were the days of dressing her up with big bows in her hair. Carly put her foot down when she was about six years old to that, and beauty pageants as well; Carly hated those with a passion.

The last beauty pageant she was in she stuck her tongue out at the judges and embarrassed Shelly to death. I tried not to laugh, but thought it was one of the funniest things I had ever seen. She stood there on the stage like an angel with bouffant hair and layers of lavender ruffles. Shelly was in the audience waving her arms around like a mad woman, helping her with the dance routine, when Carly suddenly stopped. Her tongue came out, followed by a farting noise. Then she walked right off the stage. The look on the judges' faces was hilarious. Shelly wasn't amused, and let Carly know it.

I remember we all went out to eat that night and John met us after he got off work. The kids were standing in the buffet line and Carly kicked Tyler in the shins because the boys were teasing her about her makeup and hair. Shelly yelled at Carly, but John told her Tyler deserved it. "If he can't take it, he shouldn't dish it out."

Shelly said, "I wish Jared were more like you John. He couldn't even be bothered to come and meet us for dinner." Shelly had already told me that things were so bad she was ready to call a lawyer and start divorce proceedings, so I wasn't surprised that he didn't show up.

John looked uncomfortable with the comment. I smiled, glad he was such a great husband and father.

Chapter 19

I finally told Mrs. Jenkins the news about my father because I was dying to talk to someone about it. All she could say was, "Yer a-joshin' me!"

"I'm serious. My whole life is nothing but a lie, Mrs. Jenkins. What do you think I should do?" I was fanning my face with some of the junk mail I had brought her that was lying on the table. It was a scorcher, one of the hottest of the summer.

"Lordy Mercy, girl, lemme me think a minute." We sat there rocking away, batting the flies when she finally said, "I think ya need to talk to him."

"Really? I don't know. What if he gets mad and doesn't believe me? What if he's horrible, or a crazy person, and I'm better off not knowing him?" I began chewing my nails just imagining him slamming the door in my face. Finding out you had an adult child might be a little overwhelming.

"What if he's real nice, Josie? Maybe this could turn out to be a real blessin' in yer life." She slowly rocked in her rocker looking thoughtful.

"You think so?" I wanted to believe that, but I was scared.

"Do fat babies fart?" I couldn't help but laugh. "Now, I know yer nervous, Josie, but you'll regret it ifin' ya don't."

"Maybe. Pray for me."

"Always do. How's that feller of yorn? You two talk yet?"

"Yeah. He said it only happened one time, and that he still loved me...blah, blah, blah." I rolled my eyes as if "only one time" made a difference.

Mrs. Jenkins stopped rocking and looked me directly in the eyes and said, "Take my advice, girlie girl. It ain't a deal breaker, 'cause sometimes it takes sumpin' like that to bring ya closer together. Just ask Bert."

"Well, I'd love to sit and chat with you all day, but I guess I better get busy." We both looked up at the same time when we heard gravel crunching on the driveway. Preacher Godsey was pulling in, driving his old silver Buick. I looked surprised, but somehow Mrs. Jenkins didn't.

"What a surprise! Preacher Godsey's come a-callin'." I rolled my eyes and wondered how I could sneak out.

The preacher got out of his car and walked towards the porch. He took off his hat once he was standing in the shade. He wasn't a very big man, but his voice was deep and melodious. He could belt out any hymn and give Alan Jackson a run for his money. "How do, ladies. Mighty hot day."

"You can say that again. I'm gonna wilt right off this here porch soon. How's Myrtle?" Mrs. Jenkins was fanning her face with some of the junk mail.

"Much better, Mrs. Jenkins, and thanks for askin'. This hot, dry weather is good for her arthritis." The preacher turned my way. "We've been missing you and John in church, Josie. Hope you're farin' well." Before I could respond he said, "John came the other night and did some work for me at the parsonage. Fine young man. Wouldn't take a dime."

In surprise I said, "He did?"

"Sure did. Even stayed for dinner. Had a nice long talk before he went on home."

I put my hands on my lap and looked down. "I guess you both had a lot to talk about."

Mrs. Jenkins stood up. "I gotta cake in the oven. I better go check on it." She was gone before I could even comment on her leaving, or how fast she was doing it.

After she left, Preacher Godsey sat down in Mrs. Jenkins vacated seat. "Yes'm, we sure did—have a lot to talk about, that is."

"So I guess I'm just supposed to forgive and forget, then. Is that right?" I looked up, but Preacher Godsey shook his head.

"Josie, nobody would ever think less of you if you didn't take John back. Sometimes forgivin' is a whole lot easier than forgettin'. Some of us just can't do it."

"That's exactly right, Preacher Godsey. I can't ever forget it, even if I could forgive him. I know God says we should forgive, but I'm just not there yet."

"Ain't easy, that's fer sure."

"My heart is broke."

"Your heart will mend, eventually. Can't do it on your own, though. You been trying to handle this on your own?"

I shrugged my shoulders. "It's embarrassing."

He shook his head. "Can't do it without God's help." Preacher Godsey took my hand. "Josie, it's up to you whether you give John another chance, but you need to put it in God's hands. God can work miracles. I remember the day I married you two. Didn't think he would ever stop kissin' ya when I pronounced you man and wife."

"We haven't kissed in a long time."

"Just remember what I said. God can work miracles. You've got to take one day at a time." I smiled and squeezed his hand. Sometimes words weren't enough to show your thanks.

That evening, I thought long and hard about what Preacher Godsey said. First of all, I decided not to call a lawyer...yet. I wasn't running back to John, but I also wasn't ready to get a divorce. I was still furious with him and couldn't imagine ever forgiving him, but I would do what the preacher and Mrs. Jenkins said: take one day at a time. I also decided to call my real father. Maybe talking to him on the phone first would be easier. If he wanted nothing to do with me, fine—but just maybe he would like to know he had a daughter. They only way I would know was to take the first step.

Chapter 20

L ife was flying by at an alarming rate. The boys were growing up extremely fast; it seemed like yesterday when they were running around in diapers. Tyler was in high school and Matt was in his first year of college. I was so proud of both my boys. The day Matt graduated from high school, we all celebrated. I couldn't help but cry and wish it wasn't going by so fast, but I knew it was pointless to wish for something that couldn't be. What would I do when Tyler left too? John was looking forward to the empty nest and having the house to ourselves. "Just think, Josie; you can carry on all you like and not worry about the boys hearing." He grinned but I just rolled my eyes.

"You'd like that wouldn't you?" I put my hands on my hips and looked saucily at him. "I could holler, 'Oh, John, right there, baby! Give me all ya got, big boy!'"

"Now that would be interesting. It's a date!" Taking me by the hips, John pulled me against him and kissed me on the forehead. "I have a feeling I'm going to enjoy growing old with you." As our lips met the phone began ringing. I started to pull away, but John held me tight.

"I have to get it, John. Mom went to the doctor today and she told me she would call me as soon as she got home." John gave me an exasperated look, but let me loose.

I ran to the phone and picked it up. "Hello?"

"Hello, sweetheart. I'm home." Although she tried to sound upbeat, I could tell that she sounded tired. She had found a lump in her breast the week before, and went to the doctor to get the results from her mammogram.

"Well, what did they say?"

"It's not good, sweetie. They think it's the cancer. I'm going to have surgery next Monday to remove the lump. I'm lucky to have it so soon."

"Oh, no. I'm coming over, Mom."

"All right. See you in a minute."

As I put the phone down, I looked at John with fear in my eyes. "They think its cancer. She's having surgery Monday. John, I can't lose my mom!"

"If she's having surgery, they'll take out the lump and that will be it. I'm sure of it."

I walked into John's arms and we held each other tight. "I hope you're right." After a few moments, I said, "I'm going over there. I'll be back in a bit, okay?"

"Sure. Take your time."

I ran all the way over and was out of breath by the time I reached the house. Mom and Dad were both sitting in the living room, looking like their world had ended. It was dusk, and the room was already getting dark. I started turning on the lamps to bring some light in the room and then sat next to Mom. Putting my arm around her, I said, "It's going to be okay, Mama. They'll take it out and that will be the end of it."

"I hope so, Josie." She tried to smile, but I could tell she was really worried.

"Have you told Mary?"

"She came by the doctor's office while I was there so she could hear the diagnosis for herself."

I looked at Dad, who was staring into space. "You okay, Dad?"

He jumped, as if he was startled that I was even there. Gruffly he said, "I'm fine. And your mom is going to be fine, too."

I looked at Mom and said, "I'll take Monday off so I can go with you to the hospital."

Patting my hand, she said, "You don't have to do that, dear. Mary is going to be there."

"Of course I'm going to be there. I wouldn't be anywhere else." I felt so helpless, but at least I could be there for her. "Try not to worry, Mama. Things are a lot different than they used to be."

"I know. I'll be fine. It's just that the shock hasn't worn off yet." I nodded and smiled.

"Have you eaten dinner?"

"No. I'm really not hungry." I really couldn't blame her there. Who could eat after they just found out they probably had cancer? Food was the last thing on your mind.

"Dad? Are you hungry? You want me to fix you something to eat?"

He didn't speak, just shook his head no. Feeling frustrated, I turned the television on and tried to find something upbeat. Anything would be better than this horrible silence. I found a game show that they usually liked to watch, and we all sat there looking at it but not really paying much attention. When I couldn't stand it anymore, I got up and said, "I better go now. I've got a roast in the crock pot. Call me if you need anything, Mama, all right?"

"I will, sweetie. Please don't worry. I'll be fine."

"Okay. I love you so much." I hugged her tight, then quickly walked out of the house before she saw me crying. All the way home I sobbed and prayed that my mom would be okay. John was standing on the porch with a concerned look on his face. I ran into his arms and cried until I had no tears left.

The rest of the week and weekend seemed to drag by and I thought Monday would never make an appearance. It finally came, and we were all on pins and needles. Mary and I were waiting nervously for the doctor to let us know that the surgery was over. By the time he came to the waiting room, we were exhausted with worry. He told us that it was worse than they thought. They had removed what they could, but they couldn't get it all; some of it was even in her lymph nodes. Her breast had to be completely removed, but she was resting comfortably. Mary asked about further treatment and he said that after a couple of weeks she could start chemo, followed by radiation if she was strong enough. There were no guarantees, but she wouldn't have a chance without it.

After he left, I looked at Mary and said, "She'll be okay, right Mary?" I could tell by the look on her face that she wasn't so sure.

"We can only pray at this point. If it's in her lymph nodes..." Mary just shook her head and couldn't continue. I sat back in the chair and started crying. What would she say when she found out her breast was gone and they still didn't get all the cancer? I heard horrible stories about chemotherapy, and that it was sometimes worse than the disease. I knew I had to stay strong for Mom to help her through this. She was going to need all the support she could get, and I couldn't wimp out on her now. My mom had always been there for me, and I would be there for her.

Chapter 21

It took a few days, but I finally got the nerve to pick up the phone and dial the number for David M. Murray. I waited until about seven o'clock at night, figuring that would be the best time to call. Hopefully he wouldn't be at work, eating dinner, or in bed. I was in my bedroom with the cordless so Mary wouldn't hear me.

"Hello?"

"Is this David Murray?" My body was shaking and I could hear the quiver in my voice.

"Yes. Who is this?"

"This is Josie Carrier." I waited in silence for a few seconds and then said, "You probably don't know me, but..."

"I know who you are, Josie."

In shock, I sat down on the bed. "You do?"

"I sure do."

I was stunned and speechless. He knew me? My heart was racing.

"I've been waiting for you to contact me for a long time. Would you like to meet and talk?"

"Y...yes, I would."

"Do you know where I live?"

"Yes."

"I thought so. Was that you parked in front of my house last Sunday?"

"Yes." This had to be the strangest conversation of my whole life. I didn't know what I had expected, but it wasn't this. "Can I come over tomorrow night, or would you rather meet somewhere else?"

"Here would be fine. Come any time."

We decided to meet at six o'clock. What was I doing? This was absolutely crazy. I had to get out of the house. My head was aching again and instead of taking more ibuprofen, I decided to go for a walk. It was a beautiful night, and the stars were so bright I felt as if I could reach up and grab one. I thought about my mom and the pain she must have felt. I looked up and whispered, "Why didn't you tell me, Mama? Why did you keep this a secret all those years?" I had so many questions, and I hoped that maybe I could find out some of the answers the next night.

I looked towards the cabin and saw a faint light on the porch. Suddenly I had an overwhelming desire to go home. I missed my house, my bed, and John so much it hurt. John had been a part of my life for so long that not having him there left a huge void. The dogs saw me before John did, and were nuzzling me excitedly. John stood up from the rocker he had been sitting in and watched me as I slowly walked towards him and up the porch steps.

"Hey, John." John didn't answer, but stood and looked at me as if I would disappear at any moment. "Can I talk to you about something?"

John nodded. I closed my eyes, took a deep breath and said, "This is crazy...but I found out last week that my dad is not really my dad." John looked confused so I told him the whole story of finding my birth certificate, looking my father's name up in the phone book, driving by his house, and then talking to him on the phone. I started crying and said, "I don't know...maybe this is a mistake and I should just let it go. I'm so confused."

"Of course you are." John pulled me towards him and wrapped his arms around me. I knew I should walk away, but I couldn't. I felt John's hand caress my hair and his lips kiss the top of my head. "I wish you had told me before." For a moment I forgot everything but the safe feeling of his touch and I relaxed, putting my arms around his waist. We stood that way for a while, taking comfort from each other and listening to the sounds of the night. I heard John whisper, "Josie..." I looked up, which was a mistake. I couldn't resist those eyes, those beautiful green eyes that always brought me to my knees. His lips met mine tentatively at first, and when he felt no resistance, they became more urgent. I couldn't fight anymore and gave in because it felt so right. I would worry later; right now I just wanted to feel again. Our kisses became deeper and deeper until I could no longer stand.

Taking my hand, John pulled me in the house and towards the bedroom. As we stood next to the bed, John brought my hand to his lips and said, "I love you." I didn't want to think about love at that moment. All I could think about was the ache between my thighs and I knew John could take care of it. In desperation I started taking off my clothes, telling him to hurry because I knew my common sense could return at any moment.

I almost whimpered as John came to me, his heavy-lidded eyes filled with desire so strong it made me moan with anticipation. We were desperate, clinging to each other as if it were our last hours on earth. As we became one again, I felt so much relief; the heavy burdens I had been carrying were lifted, making me feel light as a feather. I listened to John's heavy breathing for a moment after, but then reality started showing its ugly face once again. John was on top of me and his heaviness was beginning to suffocate me. His lips were on my neck and his breath was hot. I could feel myself beginning to panic so I said, "Get up John. I need to go." John lifted his head, looking at me in surprise. He rolled over so I jumped up and started putting my clothes on. Once I was dressed, I stopped at the door and said, "I'm sorry. This shouldn't have happened."

John sat up and started rubbing his face with his hands. "What do you mean? Why?"

"Because I'm still mad, that's why!" I turned and ran out of the house.

All the way home I thought about how stupid I was. How could my judgment lapse like that? I stomped down the path in frustration, and was almost to the farmhouse when I realized my headache was gone.

Chapter 22

If my mother survived the chemo, it would be a miracle. She was so small and thin she couldn't afford to lose one more pound. Her hair was falling out in clumps, leaving bald patches all over her head. Shelly came over and cut the rest of it off, so she started wearing the bright colorful scarves I bought for her to keep her head warm. Most days, she didn't have the strength to get out of bed. Just like I promised, I hardly left her side. I took off as much work as I was allowed and spent most every hour making sure she knew she wasn't alone. I only went home to sleep, falling in the bed exhausted every night. Poor John and Tyler had to learn to fend for themselves. I did the best I could, but I knew my mom needed me more.

We were all glad when Mom had her last chemo treatment. Mary assured me that she would begin to feel better once the poison was out of her system, and she would slowly gain her strength back. Thankfully Mary was right, and we finally began to have some hope that my precious mother would get better. It was like a miracle, seeing the life come back to her face; my heart would soar when she smiled. I was worried about my father, though. He was beginning to forget the simplest things. He was forever losing his keys and began repeating himself often. I didn't say anything to Mom, but one day she said, "Have you noticed anything different about your father?"

"He's been a little absentminded lately, but it's probably just because he's been worried about you." I didn't want her to worry; she had enough on her mind.

Concern was etched across her face. "I hope you're right."

"Of course I'm right! Look at me...Mrs. Jenkins fussed at me the other day because I accidentally put a piece of her mail in Mr. Thompson's mailbox. She told me to 'quit fiddle-fartin' around,' because Mr. Thompson didn't need to know her beeswax. It wasn't even anything important, just junk mail." I rolled my eyes.

Mom started laughing and said, "That sounds like Mrs. Jenkins. You know she doesn't mean it, don't you?"

"Of course. She asks about you all the time, by the way."

"She's a gem. Next time you see her, thank her for the wonderful cakes. Tell her I'm getting better, and that I'm going to beat this thing."

I smiled because I knew that having a great attitude was half the battle with a disease like cancer. It would be a rough road, but she could and would fight it with every breath of her body. I was so proud of her and prayed every day that God would not take her from us.

Slowly, things started getting back to normal. Mom felt better every day, and the doctors wanted her to begin radiation treatments as soon as she could. John complained about my dad, telling me that he couldn't keep him from over-feeding the animals. He would feed them two and three times because he forgot that he had already fed them. I made excuse after excuse for him, but deep down I knew something wasn't right. Even Mary commented about how he would ask her about the same things over and over again.

I was guilty of ignoring my father's forgetfulness because I was more concerned about Mom. Although everything seemed so much better, I still worried that it would get worse again. I tried my best to concentrate on today and not worry about tomorrow. It was easier said than done.

Mom had been doing well. For a while, we just tried to help her become stronger before radiation treatments, but the cancer soon came back with a vengeance. The doctors told her she could have chemo again, but it probably wouldn't help and she would be miserable in the process with no quality of life. Knowing I was going to lose her was breaking my heart. I tried to stay upbeat around her, but at home I was a wreck. I was sinking deeper and deeper into depression. John tried to help, but I just pushed him away. I was mad at the world, and especially God for not giving me a miracle.

Towards the end, Mom apologized for leaving Mary and me. "I'm so sorry, girls. I don't want to go, but I guess it's just my time. Your father will need you both, so please watch after him." She had finally accepted that she was going to die, but tried so hard to be brave.

I patted her hand and said, "Don't worry, Mama. Just rest."

"I don't want it to be a burden on you. I wish things were different. He's getting worse every day and refuses to go to the doctor." I wanted to shout at her to stop worrying about Dad.

Mary took Mom's other hand. "I'll make sure he goes to the doctor, Mom. We'll take care of him."

She closed her eyes and replied, "I know." Drawing strength from us, she said, "I love you both so much. I wasn't always perfect, but I did the best I could. Please remember that." I crawled in the bed with her and thought no mom was ever better or more perfect.

We found out soon after that the cancer had spread to her lungs. What began as a nagging cough soon became uncontrollable fits accompanied by blood. I wondered if God loved us so much, how could He let someone as sweet and good as my mother suffer like that? I knew that trials and tribulations were supposed to bring you closer to God, but for me it was doing the opposite.

I wanted to shout at God. I was angry: enraged that He could allow such a wonderful person to suffer when there were so many wicked people out there. They walked around without a care in the world while my mother was gasping for her last breaths. She would die and leave an empty void, while they were wasted space.

I tried to hide my hate, especially in front of her, but it was eating me up. I knew she was dying and that it was only a matter of time. How could I go on after she left me? I didn't think I would be able to handle the pain of losing her.

One early morning, I was helping her to the bathroom when she lost consciousness. Mary had warned me that it might happen, and told me to call 9-1-1 immediately. Mama died two days later; I felt the life leave her body. I didn't cry because I knew I couldn't stop if I did. Instead, I let a numbness take over my body. I knew that was the only way I would survive.

After my mother's funeral, I felt like a zombie going through the motions of life. I delivered the mail and then came home. Knowing my mother was never coming back was surreal. Sometimes I would pretend she was still alive, listening to her voice in saved phone messages that I couldn't bring myself to erase.

Dad was getting worse, and Mary moved in with him because it wasn't safe for him to be alone anymore. I would sit with him sometimes for Mary, but often resented the fact that he was still living and my sweet, precious Mama was dead. I never told anyone how I felt. I didn't want people looking at me funny, or judging me. They had no clue what I was going through.

Shelly told me I needed to go to the doctor because I was suffering from depression. Maybe I was, but who wouldn't be depressed after their mom died? I wanted to deal with it on my own, not be on some medication with side effects that were worse than depression. For the first time in my life, I was getting migraines and could barely function when they were at their worst. Sometimes they would last for a day, sometimes two or three. John ended up spending more and more time in the barn, only coming in to eat and sleep. I really didn't care; all I wanted to do was sit and stare at the television. It didn't matter what was on because I only wanted the noise; I couldn't stand silence. Sometimes I would sleep in the living room so I could leave the television on all night. If I went to bed, John would want something I couldn't give him. And I didn't know why, but I didn't want him to touch me anymore. I didn't want anyone to touch me.

Tyler was getting ready to start college. In a way, I was glad. That was one less thing I had to be concerned about. The boys were the only two people I tried to fool, because I didn't want them to worry about their mom. Putting on an act could be so exhausting, though.

Instead of getting better, day by day things were getting worse. Maybe Shelly was right, I admitted; maybe I did need to see a doctor. Even Mrs. Jenkins said I was on a downhill slide. I told her she was all the therapy I needed. She told me, "Good golly, Molly! Yer like that poor squirrel in the road that's been run over so many times his body's flat as a flitter, but his tail's still wavin' for help."

I guess Mrs. Jenkins was right. Maybe I did need to wave for help. I couldn't sit and watch mindless television forever. I needed more than day after day that consisted of just putting one foot in front of the other. I still missed my mom, but realized I needed to get on with my life. I knew she wouldn't want me to continue "living" my life like I had been. I had a husband and two children who needed me.

John was becoming aloof, but how could I blame him? I couldn't count the number of times I pushed him away. Even the boys didn't come home nearly as much as they used to. I knew they had their own lives, but I also knew that being around me was depressing.

Shelly stopped calling me. It was weeks before I realized I hadn't talked to my best friend. I needed her now, but I felt so guilty for pushing her away. Why did I push everyone away when I needed them the most? I knew I it was time to make some changes in my life, but how? I didn't need a therapist to tell me what I already knew.

PART 2:

New Beginnings

Chapter 23

I was shaking like a leaf, trying to get the courage to knock, when David opened the door. We just stared at each other; it was too hard to speak. I could already see the resemblance, and knew where Tyler and I got our blonde hair. David shook his head and said, "Where are my manners? Come on in. I'm sorry; it's just a little strange." I walked in the living room and noticed right away that no woman lived in this house. There were no flowers, pictures, or feminine touches anywhere. It was clean, neat, and tidy, though. For some odd reason, that gave me comfort. I could tell he was a Hokies fan.

"Sit down. Would you like something to drink? I have some bottled water, or I could make some fresh coffee." He seemed as nervous as I was. I could see the tremor in his hands.

I nodded and said, "Yes, water would be great; thank you." I looked around the room and saw a cat curled up on cat tree in the corner.

He came back in the living room carrying two bottles of water and gave me one of them. Sitting down in a well-worn recliner, he noticed I was looking at his cat. "That's my cat, Lou. Showed up one day and never left." Lou looked up and stretched. "I guess you have a lot of questions for me."

I took a deep breath and smiled nervously. "Yeah, I'm just a little overwhelmed right now."

"I'm sure, Josie. How long have you known?"

"Not long. I found my birth certificate in my parent's attic a few weeks ago. When I saw your name... I couldn't believe it. I've been in shock ever since."

"I want you to know, Josie, that I loved your mother very much. I wanted to marry her and be your father in every way, but it just wasn't meant to be." After taking a drink of water, David continued. "Sarah just couldn't leave your dad. I know she loved me, but things were different back then. Getting a divorce wasn't as common as it is today."

"Did my dad know? I mean, I would ask him, but he's in the later stages of Alzheimer's and his mind is long gone." I knew the answer before he told me, but I had to hear it for my peace of mind. He had always treated me differently. Maybe he didn't mean to, but he did.

"Yes. He begged her not to leave him, promising he would raise you as his own. I hope he kept his promise." David looked at me, waiting for me to confirm it.

"He was never mean to me, but I knew he didn't love me like my sister. Mom made up for it, though. She loved me enough for both of them." For some reason I smiled, wanting him to know that it was okay.

"I want you to know that what happened between your mom and me...it... Sometimes you just meet someone, and it's fate. We fought it so hard." David shook his head, and I could see his eyes were moist. "I was married as well, but I loved your mom more than my own life. I would have done anything for her, but she only wanted me to let her go. So that's what I did."

Seeing the heartbreak in his eyes, I couldn't help letting my own tears out, falling fast. For a long time, we just sat there trying to get ahold of our emotions. "I just don't understand why she couldn't tell me the truth, especially when she knew she was dying."

Shaking his head, David said, "I don't know. I wondered the same thing, and thought I might hear from you after she died. I made a promise to her that I wouldn't contact you, that I wouldn't tell you the truth. When I saw you Sunday, I thought I was seeing things. I had given up

hope that we would ever know each other. My wife and I never had children, and knowing I had a daughter I couldn't contact broke my heart."

We sat in silence, thinking about all the time we had lost. Shaking
my head, I said, "Isn't this absolutely bizarre? I can't believe I'm sitting
here talking to you and you're my father. My father! My life has turned
upside down."

"I can't imagine. I guess it hasn't been the best time for you."

I rolled my eyes and said, "You can't imagine." I wasn't about to get
into all my other problems. He would probably run as fast as he could.

"Josie, I would really love to be a part of your life. I don't want to
push you or scare you, but I've waited for this for so long. I promise you,
I'm not crazy. I just want to be your dad." He looked so earnest, and a
piece of my heart melted. I had a small glimpse of why my mother fell in
love with him.

"I'd like that too." I grinned and said, "And to think...I was scared
to death that you wouldn't want anything to do with me. Thank you."

"For what?"

"For being so nice, and not weird or anything."

"You know, you're so much like your mama. When you smile, it's like
she's here in this room."

I was trying so hard not to cry again, but hearing those words broke
the dam that I had built in my mind. Tears began streaming down my
face so fast that David looked alarmed. He jumped up and grabbed a few
tissues, thrusting them towards me with shaking hands. "It's okay, Josie.
Please don't cry."

"I...I know, but I miss her *so much.*" I hiccupped, not sure if he under-
stood a word I was trying to say.

David nodded. "I know. I miss her too."

When I finally was able to get ahold of myself, I stood up and said,
"Thank you for everything. I appreciate it so much."

David stood up as well. "I hope... I mean, can I see you again?"

In relief I said, "Yes. I would love that."

After we made plans to have dinner the following Saturday night, I left. For the first time in ages, I felt better; mostly, I felt a little bit of hope for my future. Hope was something I had given up on.

Chapter 24

"I have something to tell you, Mary." A couple of nights after I met with David, Mary and I sat down for dinner. I had made meatloaf and a salad. Red meat was plentiful at our farm; the Dickson's dairy farm down the road used some of our land and in return, we were provided with plenty of fresh beef.

"What is it?"

"The other day when I was cleaning, I went up in the attic. I found my birth certificate, and Dad is not my real dad." Mary didn't say anything. She only sat there, but I could tell she wasn't surprised. "You already knew, didn't you?"

"Yes. I found it a few months ago."

"Why didn't you tell me?"

"It wasn't my place to tell you." I looked at Mary, who continued eating without glancing up. She acted like it wasn't a big deal and it infuriated me. Sometimes I wondered if it was even worth it. I got up and emptied the remainder of my food into the trash, then began washing the dishes.

Mary eventually followed me into the kitchen. "I don't know why you're so upset with me. It wasn't any of my business." After she placed her dishes in the sink, she picked up a dish towel and began drying a plate. She still had on her gray scrubs. Gray and black were the only colors she ever wore.

I turned and looked at her with frustration. "Mary, you're my *sister*! It *is* your business! You know, I'm getting so sick and tired of you hating me. I've tried and tried to get close to you, but you always put up a brick wall. What is your problem?"

"Just because we're sisters doesn't mean we have to be best friends, Josie." Mary rubbed a particular spot on a fork hard, as if I didn't get it clean enough when I washed it. "And I don't hate you."

I grabbed the fork out of her hands and threw it back in the sink. Water splashed the ceramic frog holding the scrub pad. Most everything in the house was exactly the way Mom had left it. Soapy tears rolled down the frog's nose and into its big mouth. I took a deep breath and closed my eyes, wondering how two sisters could be so different.

"You don't have to be my best friend, Mary, but maybe you could act like you liked me just a little."

It was Mary's turn to roll her eyes. "Don't be so dramatic, Josie. We're just two different people. I don't look for butterflies and rainbows every day like you."

My mouth fell open. "Butterflies and rainbows?"

Mary took the dried plates and placed them in the cabinet. "Yes. You're like a child. You're happy one day, and then when things don't go your way, you're sad and moping around like the world has ended." She finally turned and looked at me. "Life sucks sometimes. People live, and then they die. You can't change it; you just have to accept it and move on. I miss Mom as much as you, and it kills me to see Dad the way he is. But I can't change it, so I do the best I can. Don't judge me if I don't hug everyone and tell them I love them a hundred times a day."

Mary threw her towel on the counter and walked out of the kitchen while I stood there with my mouth hanging open. I took the towel and began drying the rest of the dishes, muttering to myself. "Butterflies and rainbows! I would rather hug someone than stand there like a tree stump with a scowl on my face." The phone rang, but I was too mad to pick it up so I let Mary answer it.

Mary hollered from the living room, "It's for you, Josie."

Wiping my hands on the towel and grumbling to myself, I picked up the phone and said, "Hello."

"Hey, Josie." It was John. My face turned red as I thought about my lapse in judgment. How could I be so weak and sleep with John? "Look, I was wondering if we could go out to dinner Saturday night and talk."

I was feeling grumpy after my conversation with Mary, so I told him very bluntly, "I can't. I have plans and I don't want to break them." I wouldn't give him the satisfaction of telling him what they were. *Let him guess*, I thought. If he thought the worst, then that was his misfortune.

After several long seconds of silence, John said, "I see." I could hear the frustration in his voice, but he still refused to say anything. "Well, I hope you have a great time!" I heard the phone click and smiled, hoping he was jealous. Served him right.

I turned off the kitchen light and walked through the living room. Mary was sitting on the end of the couch doing her crossword puzzle. The lamp beside her was the only light on. Dad was staring mindlessly at the television. Some old western was on. He'd probably watched it a hundred times already.

"I'm headed to bed." Under my breath I muttered, "I think there's a rainbow or butterfly upstairs calling my name."

Mary never looked up but I thought I heard her mumble, "Maybe a unicorn will be on your bed too."

As I walked up the old creaky steps, I remembered a time when Mary and I had a fight over a stray puppy that had showed up at the farm. He was so ugly he was cute. Long, gangly legs and wiry, patchy hair didn't help his looks much. I wanted to name him Chewy for his tendency to chew everything but the kitchen sink; Mary wanted to name him Bandit for his penchant for stealing things he liked to chew and hiding them in random places.

There was an old dog house in the yard next to the barn. I painted a small sign with the name *Chewy* on it and placed it on the house. I was proud of my sign so when I saw that someone had painted *Bandit* over it the next day, I took offense. Of course, I tattled to Mom; Dad would take Mary's side. I told her how I worked so hard on the sign, and that Mary had painted over it. Mom said the evil dog should really be called Satan. He'd dug up some of her vegetables in the garden, which didn't sit well with her.

After Mom called Mary, we all sat down and resolved the whole matter. We decided to call him Chewy Bandit. Of course, I still called him Chewy and Mary still called him Bandit, but we were both satisfied. Mom always had a way of making everything better. I could just hear her telling me in her sweet voice that it was okay to chase butterflies and rainbows, and that I should also be patient and understanding with Mary because she was dealing with life the best she knew how.

Once I was upstairs, I walked to the window of my bedroom. The curtains that Mom had made were still hanging. They matched the quilt, and both had all of my favorite colors. Squares of soft lavenders, yellows, pinks, and blues were sewn together with her special love. In the soft light of my bedside lamp, I noticed the tiny purple butterflies in the print squares, causing big, fat tears to roll down my cheeks. "I miss you so much, Mama!" My hands grabbed each panel of the curtains and squeezed. "Please help me; I don't know what to do." I thought of my real father, and wondered what she would think of us getting to know each other. I also thought of John. Would she want me to forgive him? Can a marriage survive that kind of betrayal?

A loud banging downstairs startled me out of my daze. Before I could even leave my bedroom, Mary yelled. "Josie, John's at the door."

I ran down the stairs and almost tripped on the magazine rack next to my father's chair, stubbing my toe. "Ow!" I grabbed my toe and rubbed it. "Good grief! Would it hurt to turn on a few lights around here?"

"I can see just fine. John seems pretty upset, though. Better go see what he wants before he wakes up the neighbors."

Since our nearest neighbor was at least a half mile down the road, I wasn't too worried. I hobbled to the kitchen door and peeked out the window. John had his back to the house, standing there with his hands on his hips. He did look pretty mad. I opened the door and closed it quietly behind me.

I whispered furiously, "What are you doing, John, banging on the door like that?"

John was shaking he was so agitated. His fists were balled up as if he was ready to punch something. "Who do you have plans with, Josie?"

"None of your business, and keep your voice down!"

Pointing to his chest, John yelled, "It is my business! You're still my wife!"

I was in total shock. I had never seen John act this way. Of course, I had never given him any reason to be jealous. Part of me wanted to carry this thing as far as I could, just to see what he would do, but I knew I couldn't. Maybe I should mention that I was still thinking of calling Kyle Richardson.

But in the end, I couldn't. "It's not what you think, John. I'm meeting my father so we can talk some more." It was almost comical to see the anger drain from his face and be replaced by relief.

"Now I really feel like an idiot." I covered my mouth so he couldn't see my smile. Sitting down on one of the rocking chairs, he looked as if his angry burst of energy had depleted him completely. He said, "So I take it the meeting went well?"

I sat down next to him. "It was wonderful. He is the nicest man! He's wanted to be my father since I was born, but Mama wouldn't let him. We still have a lot to talk about, so we decided to meet for dinner."

"I'm glad." Looking down, he said, "I'm sorry I yelled."

I was quiet for a moment. "I don't think I've ever seen you like that before."

"Yeah, well...jealousy does strange things to you."

"You were jealous?" I knew it, but I wanted to hear more.

"Crazy jealous. I've been sitting in the cabin thinking all kinds of things, and none were good." John leaned over, elbows on his knees, and held his face in his hands. "You know, thinking of you with someone else was just about more than I could take. I just can't imagine how you felt." John looked up with tears in his eyes. "If you forgave me, it would be a miracle."

I couldn't say anything. I sat on my hands to keep from going to him. It would be so easy to go back home and try to forget the whole thing, but I still needed more time.

"What about Sunday night?" John was talking so softly that I wasn't sure if I heard him correctly.

"I can't. I promised Mary I would sit with Dad." He looked so down that before I thought about it, I said, "You can come here if you want."

"Are you sure?" I wasn't, but I nodded yes.

John smiled and so did I. I wanted to stay mad at him, but it was so hard. Always had been. He forgot our tenth anniversary, and I remembered being extremely upset. I had cooked a special dinner and couldn't wait to give him the new fishing pole I'd bought for him. I couldn't find the perfect card so I made my own, telling him how happy I had been for the last ten years and how much I loved him. He came home from work in a bad mood because of some problem with a customer. Once he calmed down and noticed the wrapped pole and card, he realized what he had done. By that time, I was near tears and feeling very sorry for myself—but by the end of the night, I had forgotten that he hadn't remembered our anniversary.

I stood up and began walking towards the door. "Okay, well, goodnight. I'll see you Sunday." I wouldn't look back at John. If I did, I'd be a goner.

"Goodnight, Josie."

After I shut the door, I leaned back against it. I wondered if I was doing the right thing. I didn't want to get his hopes up—or mine, either. Could I go back to John and pretend he never slept with Shelly? No. But maybe we could start fresh. Maybe we both deserved a second chance.

Chapter 25

I met my father at a nice family restaurant in town. He was glad to see me, and my heart was overjoyed. He was such a gentleman, always opening doors or pulling out my chair. While we ate, I learned that he and his wife had divorced soon after I was born. He couldn't hide the fact that he still loved my mom. Even though he knew that my mom wouldn't leave my dad, he couldn't continue with his marriage. After dating some, he finally gave up and decided that being a bachelor wasn't so bad. At the time he and mom met, he owned a fabric store.

"It was love at first sight when I first saw Sarah. She was looking for fabric to make some kitchen curtains. I went out of my way to help her. Next, she came back for something to make a dress for Mary. Pretty soon, I knew she had feelings for me, too, the way she kept coming back.

"One day she came in and told me she wouldn't be coming back. I asked her why and she said, 'Because you know why I keep coming back here, David, and it isn't right.' I was devastated, but I didn't argue with her. Every day I hoped she would change her mind...and then one day she did. She came in looking so beautiful. I'll never forget it. My heart stopped and I knew I would do anything for her, including leaving everything and running away with her and Mary.

"She told me that her husband was going to be out of town that weekend, fishing or hunting or something like that. She wrote down directions to their farm and wanted me to come so that we could talk.

She didn't have to ask me twice! I told her anytime, anywhere, I would be there. That weekend was the best weekend of my whole entire life. It was also the last time I ever spent any time with her. The guilt just about did her in. I saw her about a year later in town and she was holding you. I knew right away that I could be your father because we didn't use protection. I asked her if you were my baby. She didn't deny it and begged me not to say anything, begged me to never tell anyone. I loved her so much and would do anything for her, so I honored her wishes, as much as it killed me to do so. I had just about given up hope that you would find me, but here we are."

It was strange, hearing about my mom this way. I tried to imagine her flirting with David, but I couldn't see it. In my eyes, my mother was perfect. Knowing she was fallible just like the rest of us was disconcerting. I couldn't help but compare Mom's affair with John and Shelly. It was a lot to think about.

There were consequences to my mom's choices. I recognized most of my life that she wasn't really happy. Did she live a life of regret by staying with dad? Did she regret that she became pregnant with me? Maybe at first, but I knew she loved me. I never doubted her love. And poor David... To love someone that much and never be able to be with her must have been horrible. What a sad, lonely life.

"Now I want to hear about you, Josie. Tell me about your life."

"Well, I've been married twenty-six years." I stopped for a second and realized that John and I had missed our anniversary. "I have two sons. One is at ETSU and one graduated last year; he's a policeman. I work for the post office delivering mail, and... Oh, I like to paint, or at least I used to. I haven't painted much lately."

"You're kidding! I like to paint too, but mostly I love woodworking. I have a shop behind the house. I'm not that good of a painter, but my mother was. She was a professional artist and sold many paintings."

"That's so cool! Do you have some of her artwork? Is she still alive?" I didn't think she would still be living but you never knew.

"No, she died a few years ago, at the ripe old age of ninety-three. I do have some artwork of hers. I would love to give you some of it, if you want it."

"Of course, I would love to have it!" I couldn't believe how well we were connecting. It was like we had been father and daughter for years instead of days. I finally had the part of me that had been missing all these years. I wasn't sure what to call him, though, and voiced my concern.

"You can call me anything you want. Don't stress about it. You can call me David, if that would be more comfortable for you."

"I want you to meet my family, but things are a little upside down right now. My husband and I are actually separated. He knows about you, but the boys don't. I need to figure out how I'm going to tell them, not that it would be a big deal. They've never been close to Dad either."

"I'm sorry about you and your husband. I hope you can work it out."

"Yeah, me too. I first blamed it all on him, but I've thought about it a lot lately and I'm starting to come to the realization that maybe it wasn't entirely his fault. I guess I have some blame too. I had my head in the clouds for so long after Mama died, but I'm starting to see more clearly now. We're supposed to meet and talk tomorrow night. If he's ready to try again, I think I am too. Hopefully we'll put it all behind us and start fresh. I've got a lot of praying to do."

"I have a feeling you'll do just that."

The whole evening was great. I thought God must have led me right to that box in the attic with my birth certificate. Meeting my real father brought new life into my soul. Maybe that new life would spread to my marriage. Could we really begin a new life, with all that had happened? Could I forgive John completely, or would his affair with Shelly always be between us?

Chapter 26

Sunday night came and I heard someone knocking on the kitchen door. I couldn't believe it, but I was actually looking forward to seeing John and talking to him. Earlier, I had freshened up and even put on a little perfume. Feeling hopeful and a little light in my step, I opened the door and smiled. He had picked some wild daisies and was holding them in his hand. That was something you didn't see very often. I wished I had a camera so I could take a picture. As if embarrassed, he handed them to me and said, "Here, these are for you."

Taking them from him, I said, "Thank you, John. They're beautiful. Come on in. Have you eaten? I have some fresh ham. I could make you a sandwich." We walked into the kitchen and I looked under the sink for a vase.

"Thanks, but I had a late lunch. I'm not hungry."

"Come on in the living room and we can talk. Dad is listening to the radio, or at least he's sitting there while the radio is on. I'm not sure if he hears anything."

Suddenly, we were both nervous and tongue-tied. I took a deep breath as John sat down on the couch. He didn't wear cologne, but I could smell my favorite soap. It had a hint of sandalwood. We both sat there silently for a few seconds, then started talking at the same time. Laughing, I said, "You go first."

"I just wanted to ask you how your dinner went Saturday night."

"Oh, John, it was wonderful. We already have a great connection. I can't believe how lucky I am to have found him. It still baffles my mind, though." I looked at Dad in his chair and shook my head.

"I'm glad. I can already see a change in you. I haven't seen you smile like that since...well, for a long time." I looked at him and realized what he said was true. I hadn't smiled in a long time.

"I know. I haven't been the easiest to live with and for that I'm sorry. You were right. Things really changed for me when Mama died, and even before that. I didn't cope very well and I pushed you away. I don't know why, either, especially when I needed you the most."

"It didn't give me the right to do what I did, though." I could still see the pain in John's eyes. I wondered if he would ever forgive himself.

"No, it didn't...but I understand now why you did it. I think Shelly knew what she was doing, and came to you when you were at your most vulnerable. She's always been jealous of what we've had, and has always looked for someone exactly like you. I guess she thought maybe the real you would be even better."

John shook his head. "If I could just go back, I would change everything."

"There's no going back, John. If we move forward, we have to try and forget the past. I've done a lot of thinking and soul searching. There have been lots of clues in the past regarding Shelly and I chose to ignore them. I've opened my eyes finally to what kind of person she is. She was my best friend and I didn't want to see what was always there. She wanted you. I'm not sure she even knows what true love is, but she wanted you and she was going to do whatever it took to get you."

John's head was down, and I saw an intense look on his face.

"This wasn't the first time she went after you, was it?"

John looked up and whispered, "No."

"John, why didn't you tell me?"

"She was your best friend. I didn't want you to be hurt. I always let her know that it was you I loved, and always would love."

I bit the corner of my lip. "Until I pushed you away."

"I don't know what the heck happened. It's like I was someone else. I don't know how to explain it."

I smiled at John. "What she didn't realize is that she was never going to be happy or satisfied, even with you. You know why?" John shook his head and I said, "Because you would never look at her the way you look at me."

John closed his eyes and big, fat tears rolled down his cheeks. I scooted over and put my arms around him, wiping the tears away. I put my lips softly on his and said, "I love you, John Carrier."

"Will you come home then? Please? I don't think I can live one more day in that cabin without you." I could see the misery in John's eyes and knew he needed me. Mrs. Jenkins was right. John sleeping with Shelly wasn't a deal breaker; it was an eye opener.

"What would you say if I told you my bags are already packed?"

"Thank you, Jesus!" John pulled me on his lap and held me close. "I promise you, Josie, you won't regret it. I will spend every day for the rest of my life making it up to you." John brought my fingers to his lips and kissed them. "I thought I had lost you forever until you came to me the other night. I thought I must have been dreaming when you showed up. Even when you left and said what you did, I knew it wasn't over."

"I can't even remember what I said."

"You said, 'Because I'm still mad, that's why.' I just knew I had some hope then."

"Why? Because I can't resist you when you look at me with those eyes? And because my knees go weak and my heart beats like crazy when you kiss me?"

"Does it?"

I smiled sheepishly and said, "Yeah." I laughed out loud and said, "You know what Mrs. Jenkins said?"

"Oh Lord! You told Mrs. Jenkins? Please tell me you didn't!"

"Well, you know her! She has a way of bringing it out of you before you even realize what you're saying!" I bit my lip in remorse. John always complained that I couldn't keep anything to myself. "Anyway, she loves you dearly and told me that it wasn't a deal breaker, and that something like this could bring us closer together."

John sighed and leaned his head against the back of the couch. "I'll never be able to look at Mrs. Jenkins again!"

I looked at my father when I heard him breathing funny. Walking over to him I put my ear to his chest and heard a faint rattling sound. I wasn't a nurse, but I knew it didn't sound right. His forehead felt a little warm, indicating a slight fever. I had noticed that lately he didn't even get up anymore to walk around the room. He just sat and stared into space. "I wish Mary would get home. His breathing doesn't sound right, and I think he has a fever."

"Where is she, anyway?"

"That's what I would like to know. She won't tell me anything. I've given up trying to understand her anymore." I will still mad about the butterflies and rainbow comment.

"You think she's on a date?" John grinned as if this would be impossible.

"Maybe she's out dancing at some bar. Sometimes I smell smoke on her clothes; that is, if she lets me get close enough."

All of a sudden, Dad began gasping, as if he couldn't breathe very well. "John, I'm scared. I'm going to call nine-one-one."

"I think you'd better."

After calling 9-1-1 I texted Mary to let her know what was going on. Once the paramedics were on their way, I felt better. "They said he probably has pneumonia. It's pretty typical for Alzheimer's patients. He'll probably have to stay in the hospital for a couple of days. Did I tell you we found a facility for him? Hopefully he'll have a room soon."

"I can't believe he's not already in a facility." I nodded, thinking the same thing.

Mary walked in the house right after the paramedics arrived. "What happened?"

I stood there watching the paramedics with my arms crossed. "They think he might have pneumonia. He's having trouble breathing and he feels like he might be running a fever."

With a troubled look on her face, Mary walked over and looked at our father as they put him on a stretcher. She gently placed her hand on his forehead. As we followed the paramedics out of the house, Mary turned and said, "There's no use all of us going. They'll admit him, then give him antibiotics and fluids intravenously. I'll go and take a vacation day tomorrow." Without waiting for a response, she continued on to her car.

"Mary!" She finally turned around and I said, "I'm going home tonight and I won't be back."

"Okay. I'll let you know what's going on." I watched her as she drove away behind the ambulance. Looking at John, I shrugged and we walked back into the house to get my things and lock up.

I sighed in relief as we walked into the cabin. "I'm glad to be home."

John placed my suitcase on the floor and walked over until he was standing in front of me. Taking my face in his hands, he said, "No one is more glad than me." I smiled and put my arms around him. With my cheek resting against his heart, I thanked God for bringing us back together. It felt so good to be held and loved again. I made a promise to myself that I would never push him away again. From this day forward, I would make sure he knew how much I loved him every day. I believed my mom somehow had a part in my new revelations, taking care of me from the grave. Realizing she was still with me gave me so much comfort and peace.

Chapter 27

Mary confirmed it the next day that dad did have pneumonia. Hopefully he would be fine, but he would definitely have to stay in the hospital for a few days. John and I both went around with smiles on our face the next few days. Mrs. Jenkins knew right away that things had changed for me, and for the better.

"What's up with you, young'un? You look as happy as a puppy with two peters!"

"Mrs. Jenkins! Where do you come up with this stuff?" I couldn't help but laugh. She could be so crude sometimes, but only she could get by with it.

"I call 'em like I sees 'em. I'm guessin' you went back home. Makin' up's always the best. Sometimes I would pick a fight with Bert just so's we could have a little more fun later." She slapped her leg and laughed so hard her false teeth almost flew out of her mouth.

I tried not to laugh but couldn't help the smile that wouldn't go away. "It's not just that. My dinner with David Saturday night was incredible. He couldn't be nicer. I do have some bad news. Dad's in the hospital with pneumonia. Mary said he'd have to stay a few days. I'm wondering if he'll ever come back home."

"That's not good. I told Bert to just shoot me if I ever get in such a shape. Ain't no benefit in livin' life like that." She shook her head and shuddered.

"I agree, Mrs. Jenkins. I wouldn't wish that on my worst enemy. Listen, I have a carload of mail waiting on me, so I better head out. Have I told you lately how much I appreciate you?"

"Aw, go on with ya! Tell John I said howdy." She giggled like a little girl, which caused me to laugh out loud.

That evening, John and I went to the hospital to check on Dad. The nurse informed us that he had been really agitated, and kept pulling the drug line out of his arm. At the moment, he was sleeping peacefully. He looked so frail, lying there, and I wondered if he was getting close to the end. *It may be too late for a nursing home now*, I worried. John and I stayed for about an hour, then left to get something to eat.

Something as simple as getting a hamburger and eating it with John made me feel happy. We acted like two teenagers, sitting there grinning at each other. I let my sandal drop off my foot. Slowly I began rubbing my toes up and down his jean-clad leg. John's eyes grew big and he whispered, "Would you cut it out?"

Trying not to laugh, I said, "Fine." I took a drink of my soda and swirled the straw with my tongue. I closed my eyes and sipped. When I opened them up John had a pained expression on his face.

"You're killing me. Either stop or hurry up and finish your hamburger."

"Okay! I'll hurry." This was too much fun. I could tell he was really bothered and knowing I did that to him was so amazing, even after all these years and everything we had been through.

"Josie? John? How are you guys?"

I looked up and saw Kyle Richardson. I could tell he was confused that we were together. Embarrassed, I said, "We're fine, Kyle. How are you?"

"I'm glad to see that you two are back together." He looked at both of us in turn and smiled.

Awkwardly John and I sat there and smiled our thanks. Kyle asked John about a job, and they talked for a few seconds. After he left, John gave me an irritated look and said, "Does everyone know our business? How in the world did he find out? When did you see him?"

"Calm down, John. I saw him in the grocery store after... I was picking up some things for Mary. He wanted me to tell you about a job he thought you would be interested in, and I told him that he would have to tell you himself because we were separated. That was it, and I haven't seen him since. Why are you so jealous all of a sudden?"

"After what?"

"What do you mean?" I knew what he meant but I was just stalling for time. I really did have a big mouth.

"You said you saw him in the grocery store after...and then you stopped. After what?"

I looked down and shook my head. "Don't make me say it." Thinking back to that day in Shelly's beauty shop made me feel embarrassed. I still couldn't believe that I confronted her in front of all those people.

"Spit it out, Josie."

Chewing the inside of my lip, I hesitated and then said, "Well...it was the first Saturday morning after we separated. I...I was really aggravated, and mad. I went to Shelly's shop." John covered his face with his hands and bent his head down. "I just wanted her to know that I was mad and that I would never forgive her."

"Did you do it privately?"

"Not exactly."

"What does that mean, Josie?"

He might as well know it all. "I confronted her in the shop, but we didn't have words until we were both in the back room. But you know how thin those walls are. I just said something about if she called herself a friend, I would hate to see my enemies. Are you happy now?"

Throwing his uneaten food on the tray, he got up and walked to the trash receptacle. I cringed when I saw Kyle watching us from his place in line to order his food. I had to run to catch up with John before he got to the truck. I opened the passenger side door and got in. John just sat there looking straight ahead. I wasn't about to apologize, even though I probably didn't use the best judgment. Hopefully he would calm down quickly. I knew he was a private person and hated other people knowing our business, but sometimes you couldn't hide everything. I was more like an open book and tended to tell more than I should, but it wasn't as if I blabbed to everyone.

He finally started the truck and we drove home in silence. As we pulled in front of the house, he turned and looked at me. "I hate this, but I don't have anyone to blame but myself." I tried to speak, but he stopped me with his fingers to my lips. "I understand. I hate that you felt you had to confront her, but I understand." Pulling me close against his warm chest, he said, "If it takes forever, I will make it up to you. I mean it, Josie. I will do whatever it takes."

I nodded, too choked up to say anything. I believed him with all my heart.

Chapter 28

Dad wasn't getting any better, and the doctors feared he didn't have much more time. Plans were made to put him in a hospice facility. He had six months to stay there, but his doctor didn't think he would last even two. I could tell Mary was emotional, but she kept her distance. I tried to go out at least every other day to sit with him. John came with me sometimes, but most of the time I told him to stay at home. He had so much to do around the farm this time of year, and I wanted to make sure he finished up his work so he could spend time with me in the evenings.

Sometimes Mary would be visiting at the same time and we would sit there saying nothing. She would work on her crosswords or needlepoint, and I would sit and stare out the window. I couldn't help but wonder what would happen to the farm when Dad died. Would Mary stay there in the farmhouse, or would she want to move? I couldn't blame her if she did. The house was old and drafty, and it needed a lot of work.

"I need to tell you something." I jumped when Mary spoke. It was as if she had read my mind. "We both know that Dad won't be here long. I haven't seen the will, but I'm sure everything will be left to both of us. I'll probably sell my half." She looked me straight in the eye and dared me to object.

I was looking at her in shock. "John and I can't afford to buy half of the farm, Mary."

"I'll offer you a fair price below market value. I know you and John don't want to split the farm up." She closed her crossword book and placed it in her bag. "I need a fresh start, Josie. I have no one else to depend on but myself. I could really use the money."

Until Mary came back to stay with dad, she never had anything to do with the farm. John had poured his whole being into working on that farm for more years than I could count. It didn't mean anything to her, but it meant the world to us. I wasn't going to argue with her, especially with Dad lying there right next to us.

"We'll worry about it when the time comes." I would not let her get to me. Standing up, I said, "I've got to get home." I walked out the door calmly, but inside I was bristling.

I told John what Mary said and he tried to calm me down.

"How can you not be upset, John, especially because of all the work you've put into this farm? How can she just sell something that has been in the family for so long?" Three generations of Taylors had worked their fingers to the bone keeping it alive and going. John wasn't a Taylor, but he loved it just as much as they did.

"Look, we'll always have our cabin and the five acres your parents gave us. That's all we need."

I think I was more upset with her whole know-it-all attitude than anything, but if John was okay with it, then I would be too. I thought about Mary going through those boxes in the attic. She was probably looking for a copy of the will. I was pretty sure that Mom had told me it was in the possession of their lawyer. She didn't tell me what was in it, but she did tell me not to worry about anything.

As I was getting ready for bed that night, the phone rang. I looked at the caller I.D. and saw that it was Shelly. She had some nerve calling our house. Did she actually think I would talk to her? As the shrill rings continued, I wondered if she even wanted to talk to me. Maybe she didn't realize I was here and was calling John. That thought made me furious. John was still outside, so I let it ring until the answering machine picked it up. I heard her voice say, "John, it's Shelly. If you're there, please call me. I really need to talk to you. I miss you." Her voice sounded anxious and pathetic. I wanted to reach through the phone and wring her neck.

Just when I thought everything was better. the sound of her voice pleading with John brought me to my knees. I couldn't stop the images of John and Shelly making love and I bent over in pain. Slowly easing myself to the bed, I began rubbing my temples trying to think of anything but them when John walked in.

In a concerned voice, he lifted my chin and said, "Hey, what's wrong?"

I just shook my head and started crying, unable to speak. Sitting next to me, John put his arm around me and made soothing noises, telling me everything would be okay.

I turned finally and grabbed his shirt. "Has Shelly been calling you?"

I could tell by the look on his face that she had. "Yes, but I keep ignoring her. I talked to her and told her it was over weeks ago. I told her I loved you. I swear I haven't spoken to her since."

I didn't know why, but I had a bad feeling about it. "She just called again. Has she left you a message telling you what she wants?"

"Only that she needs to talk to me."

Taking a deep breath, I said, "You need to call her and find out what she wants."

"No, it's over. I'm not going to call her." John looked adamant, but I kept on.

"I'll sit next to you when you call. If you don't do this, she won't leave you alone. She needs closure, and so do we. It will be hard and uncomfortable, but then it will be done and finished. Please, John. Do it now, and get it over with." I began crying again. "I can't take it. When I heard her voice it all came back to me. You have to do it, John."

I could tell that John was mad and frustrated, but I knew he would do it. I put my arms around him and held him tight. "I love you. It will be okay."

John nodded so I got the phone and dialed the number. I could see his hands trembling as he waited for Shelly to answer. I heard his side of the conversation.

"It's John."

"I'm fine, but I want you to stop calling me."

"I told you it was a mistake. I don't want you calling me anymore."

"No, Shelly. Look, I don't know how to tell you any plainer. I'm not going to see you, not now and not ever."

John looked at me and started shaking his head and threw up his hands. I put my hand out so he gave me the phone.

I took the phone and put it to my ear. "Shelly, stop it. This is ridiculous. Stop calling him."

"Are you two back together?" I could hear the surprise in her voice.

"Yes, so stop calling and leave us alone. Do you understand me?"

"I know he cares for me. You only want him now because you're jealous," Shelly replied.

"Are you delusional, or just crazy?"

"It's not over, Josie. There's a lot you don't know. Do you know that I was his first and not you?"

My stomach dropped and all the blood drained from my face.

"It's true," Shelly continued. "Just ask him."

I closed my eyes and holding my stomach I bent over. John grabbed the phone. "What's wrong with you, Shelly? What did you say?"

"I finally told her, John. She had to know the truth, that I was your first. I know deep down you love me. You can never forget your first love."

John stood up and paced across the room. "It was never love with you, and never will be. Don't ever call here again. As soon as I hang up, I'm going to get a restraining order against you. Don't contact me or Josie. You got it?"

I could hear Shelly yelling, but John hung up on her. Looking dejected, I pulled one of the pillows from the bed and hugged it, rocking back and forth. I couldn't look at him but I whispered, "When, John? When?"

John sat back down beside me and tried to hug me but I stiffened, pushing him away. "Don't touch me! Just tell me the truth!"

He looked so dejected and hopeless I almost felt sorry for him. Almost. He stood up and placed his hands on his face, then rubbed them through his hair, leaving it disheveled. "I'll tell you everything, but I want you to remember that it meant absolutely nothing to me and I have always loved you. Only you. Okay?"

I sniffed, wiped my eyes, and nodded.

"She came to campus my freshman year. It was during finals, and I was pretty stressed. Some guys bought some beer, and I thought I would have one just to help calm me down. One led to another, and then another. I wasn't used to it so I got pretty wasted."

I looked at him in shock. "I know. Believe me, it never happened again. That was my first and last time." He sat down next to me on the bed again and rubbed his knees nervously.

"Anyway, Shelly and some girl came to our dorm room. I went to my bedroom, intending to sleep it off before I said or did something I regretted. I knew she would run straight to you, blabbing about me drinking." Shaking his head and fighting the tears that began falling down his face anyway, he continued, "Shelly followed me to my room. I told her to leave, but she said she just wanted to make sure I was okay. She was being nice and at first kept her distance. We just kept talking until I got sleepy and had to lay down on my bed. I must have dozed off; the next thing I knew, she was beside me. I swear Josie, I was thinking of you. One thing led to another, and then...then it was over."

John wiped the tears streaming down his face. "I'm so sorry, Josie." His voice broke as he continued. "I hated myself afterwards. Shelly kept saying it was nothing, that you would never find out. But I knew it, and it was killing me." John hung his head in shame, his gasping breaths the only sound in the room.

We sat on our bed in silence that seemed to go on forever. I was in shock and John looked like he was waiting for his death sentence.

"Did she stop?" I had to know. Did she come on to John over our entire marriage, with me oblivious?

John looked confused. "What do you mean?"

"I mean, did she stop there, or did she try to sleep with you again?"

"Yes. No. She did stop then, but she called me sometimes. Then, the day before our wedding, she begged me not to get married. She said she loved me and always had."

I couldn't believe it. She had acted so happy for me the day of our wedding. We laughed constantly, and she gave me all kinds of advice for our honeymoon. I cringed thinking about me telling her intimate details afterward.

"I always made it a point to not be in any room alone with her, but sometimes she would manage to corner me. I always brushed her off. Sometimes she would leave me alone for a while, but it would never last."

I shook my head in disbelief. Knowing that Shelly had lusted after my husband since before we were married was unbelievable. Not only did I live a lie with my father, I had also lived a lie with my best friend.

I let out a deep breath. "Well, I know you weren't her first." Taking a deep, cleansing breath, I said, "I know that was hard, and I appreciate you telling me. I'm going to try my best to get past it. I don't know if I can, but I'll try."

John leaned back against the pillows and brought me down with him. We held each other, listening to the clock on the wall ticking. Eventually we both fell asleep.

I had invited David over for dinner that following Saturday night. Preparing a meal and anticipating his visit kept my mind on something other than Dad or Shelly. John was going to grill some steaks, and I made baked potatoes and a salad to go with them.

David seemed to love the cabin, exclaiming over all the wood detail. We had opted for shiplap on all the walls and no sheetrock to have a more authentic feel, just like our honeymoon cabin. John came in from the back porch and I excitedly introduced them. "So this is my daughter's husband! I'm so glad to finally meet you." They shook hands. "I can't wait to meet the boys. You have any pictures?"

I showed him their senior pictures hanging in the living room, and he talked about how handsome they were. I said, "Sit down and have some ice tea while we wait on the steaks."

While John finished cooking the steaks, I told David about Dad. "He began showing signs of the disease before Mama died. She was worried about him being a burden on Mary and I. Sometimes I still can't believe she's gone."

"I would have given anything to be able to hold her hand. When I saw that she had died, I cried for a week. I even came to the funeral, and that's when I saw you." He took my hand and put it to his cheek. "Thank you, sweetheart, for finding me."

I smiled and said, "Finding you was one of the best things that has ever happened to me." We both had tears in our eyes when John walked back in with the steaks. Jumping up I began putting everything else on the table, glad to have something to do.

The whole evening was wonderful. We walked over to the barn later so David could see some of my paintings. I had them all stored in a sealed room. "I haven't done anything for a while, but I hope to get back to painting soon."

"You should, you're very talented. Your style is very similar to my mother's; it's uncanny." He looked closely at each one, studying them intently.

"You can have one if you want."

"I would love one, but there's only one problem. I can't decide!" He finally selected a painting of the pond. The trees were full of fall colors and the sun glistened on the water. "I want this one. Is this pond somewhere on the property?"

"Yeah, it's not far. I'll take you there one day."

"It's beautiful, Josie. I can't thank you enough."

After he left, I looked at John and said, "Well? What do you think?"

John just shook his head and smiled. "I think you're crazy about your father, and he seems to feel the same way about you. I like him."

"He's great, isn't he? How lucky am I, to find him after all these years?" I went on and on about David until John started yawning and I said, "Okay, I'll shut up now."

Smiling, John said, "You're fine, Josie. Talk all you want. Anything that makes you happy makes me happy."

John helped me with the dishes and once we were done, we decided to go for a ride on the four-wheeler. The blackberries and raspberries were ripe, and I wanted to pick some for a cobbler. Ricky and Lucy ran ahead of us. John had already bush hogged the trails to get them ready. We found some ripe raspberry bushes, so I got my bucket ready. I had to fight Lucy for them because she liked to put her whole mouth on the vine and chomp down. They were so sweet and juicy I couldn't blame her.

Once I got the bucket about one-fourth full, we headed up the trail for more. When we stopped, I hesitated before I got out. I took deep breath and looked at John. "I know you don't want to talk about it, but when did things change between you and Shelly?" I looked ahead because I knew it didn't matter, but for some morbid reason, I wanted to torture myself.

"Josie, don't."

"John, just tell me. If you don't, then my imagination will just make something up. And it could be a whole lot worse than what really happened."

I still wouldn't look at John, but I could hear him sighing. He turned off the engine and we sat in silence for what seemed like an eternity.

Before he said a word, he took my hand and held it. "For the record, I want to say this is a bad idea." I was silent waiting for him to continue. "She called me one day and asked me to come by the shop. Something was wrong with one of the outlets. It had a short, or something in it. I didn't want to go, but I had some free time so I went."

I squeezed his hand to let him know it was okay to continue. "When I got there Shelly was cleaning up, and everyone had already left for the day. She had made a cake and wanted me to come back and taste it to see if it was okay."

I already knew that was a lame excuse to get him in the back. How could he be so stupid? Inside I was already seething, but I sat there silently, urging him to go on with hand squeezes.

"We both sat down, and she asked about you and if you were still depressed. I told her you were having a rough time. She asked me how I was and I said I was okay. She kept saying 'I know you're not okay, John.' She said, 'I'm always here for you, no matter what.' I knew deep down that I needed to be careful with Shelly, but I...I don't know, I guess I let my guard down, and..."

"So you slept with her."

"No, not then. She called a couple of other times for different reasons. At first, we would just talk, and I was okay with that. We talked a lot about you and how we both loved you." I could tell John was struggling to go on, but I waited patiently. "Remember when we got in that bad fight one morning while we were still in bed?"

I remembered. I woke up with John behind me. He was kissing my neck, trying to pull me closer. I pulled away and told John to stop. I told him I wasn't ready, and he asked when I was going to get ready. He was tired of waiting. I remembered shouting "Maybe never!" John stomped out of the house that morning and I knew I had pushed him to his limits, but I didn't care. I also remembered that Shelly had called me that day and knew something was wrong. I had told her that John and I had a fight that morning, but didn't tell her why.

"That day, Shelly called again. This time it was the dryer vent. She could tell I was mad and frustrated. She apologized, and said she would give me a free haircut since I was looking a little scraggly." I had been cutting his hair with the clippers, but had been guilty of putting it off. I wished I hadn't, hearing that.

"Everyone was gone. I thought, what the heck? I did look pretty bad. While she was cutting my hair, she kept touching me. One thing led to another..."

"That's enough, John. Take me home."

"I told you it was a bad idea."

"I know what you said. Just take me home!"

"Damn!" John started the four-wheeler and we took off for home, leaving the dogs in a cloud of dust. I jumped out before he could even stop in front of the porch and ran in the house. I slammed the bedroom door and threw myself on the bed. I hated them both at that moment but Shelly was the worst! She had played him like a fiddle, and he fell hook, line, and sinker. Why did I make him tell me the whole sordid truth? Now the images were in my head, and I couldn't make them stop.

John waited about an hour, but he finally came to bed. I had already washed up and put on my nightgown. I was lying on my side reading, but not really retaining anything I read. I was really thinking about what I would say to him once he came to bed.

John slowly lifted the covers, as if he was waiting for me to tell him to sleep somewhere else. "I washed the berries and put them in the fridge."

I could feel him looking at me, but pretended a deep interest in my book. "Thanks."

"You said earlier to remind you about taking the pound cake out of the freezer. You want me to take it out for you?"

"Do whatever you want." I knew John was frustrated, but I couldn't stop the nastiness in my voice.

"Josie, what the heck do you want from me?"

"I want it to never have happened!"

"Well, that's not possible! I told you it was a bad idea, but you had to know all the stupid details. I wish it had never happened too! It makes me sick to think about it, much less explain it to my wife. I have no excuses, but I love you more than anything, Josie. I've loved you since we kissed that first time on the fourth of July, and I will always love you, whether you forgive me or not. It's always been you."

Out of the corner of my eye I saw John wipe a tear from his eye before he turned off the lamp on his side of the bed. He rolled over with his back to me. I put my book down and turned off my lamp, too. I slowly scooted over and wrapped my arms around him. His right hand took mine and placed it on his heart.

"I'm sorry, John."

John rolled over and gathered me in his arms. "I'm sorry too, baby." He kissed the tops of my fingers. "If I have to ask forgiveness the rest of my life, I will. Whatever it takes, I'll do it."

"I know. Just be patient with me. Have you really loved me since our first kiss?"

"Crazy in love."

"I love you too, John. Forever and ever."

Chapter 29

For the first time since I had made a scene over sitting in a different pew, John and I walked into church. I held John's hand and led him to our regular seat. As we sat down, I said, "I'll try to be better this time." John just shook his head and rolled his eyes. Sneaking a peek to my left, I noticed the Johnsons were sitting in their usual pew. Victoria was chomping her gum, scrolling on her cell phone while her mother and father looked apathetic. I laughed to myself and thought that they could maybe use a little shakeup in their lives, too.

I looked around the church at all the familiar faces. I had been going to this church all my life. Mrs. Breedlove caught my eye and smiled. She was my Sunday School teacher for many years as a child, and also a very good friend of my mother's. She prepared many meals for Mom and Dad when Mom was sick with chemo treatments. I smiled back and squeezed John's hand.

There was something so comforting in seeing all the familiar faces in our church. These were people I had known most of my life, and they had watched me grow up, marry, and have children of my own. They were good people—not perfect, but good. You could always count on your church family. They prayed for you, fed you, and loved you.

At the beginning of the service, Preacher Godsey saw us and said, "It's good to have the Carriers back with us." John and I both smiled and nodded. Preacher Godsey's lesson focused on Ephesians 6:10–18. Was it a coincidence that we were told to be "strong in the Lord" and to "stand firm?" I knew that God was with us every moment.

I thought back to the last time John and I had come to church, and remembered how unhappy I was. I couldn't believe how things had changed since that day. Even though they got worse before they got better, I had so much hope due to those changes. With God's help and John back by my side, I could face whatever else life threw at me.

Pulling out of the church parking lot, John asked me if I wanted to go to Johnson City and take Matthew and Tyler out to lunch. After I told him I did, he said, "Great. Call the boys and tell them we're coming."

John blew the horn when we pulled into the parking space right in front of their apartment, and they came walking out like they just got out of bed. I looked at them both with a smirk and said, "Late night, boys?"

Offended, Matthew protested, "I worked late last night!"

"What's your excuse, Tyler?" Tyler just grinned, then yawned.

John headed for his favorite barbecue place, and we all went in and sat down. John finally looked at Tyler and said, "If you yawn one more time, you can go sit in the car while we eat." Looking chagrined, Tyler sat up straighter and did his best to wake himself up.

Matthew rubbed Tyler's head and said, "Tyler had a hot date last night. I think he's in *luuvv*."

Tyler shook his hand off and said, "Shut up!"

"Who is it?" I always perked up when it came to the boys' love lives. Usually I stayed in the dark, because they both keep their private lives to themselves. They had never dated anyone long enough for me to get to know them.

Stifling a yawn, Tyler quickly looked at his father to see if he noticed. "Just a girl."

"I hope it's a girl. What's her name?" Looking at all three of their perturbed expressions, I said, "Oh, never mind."

Matthew sat up straighter in his seat and said, "Oh, by the way, guess who came to see us last Sunday?"

John and I both asked, "Who?"

"Carly's mom. She was acting all funny and stuff, and wanted to take us out to lunch. Not wanting to pass up a free meal, we went—but she was weird. She was trying to act like she was our mother, or something." John and I both just sat there, stunned and speechless.

Tyler said, "Carly said she was losing it. She's been acting crazy lately."

In a serious, somber voice, John said, "Look, boys; do me a favor and stay away from her."

The boys looked at us, confused. Matt asked, "What's going on?"

John just sat there, so I said, "Don't ask boys, just do as your father says."

The rest of the meal was finished with little conversation. I could tell that John was upset and agitated. The boys were quiet and thoughtful. On the way back home, I said, "What are we going to do, John? Do you think we should go to the police? Do you think she means to cause trouble?"

"I have no freakin' idea. I want to choke the life out of that woman!" His hands were gripping the steering wheel and his foot was getting heavier and heavier on the gas pedal.

"John, please slow down." Putting my hand on his arm, I rubbed it, trying to soothe him in the only way I could. Would things ever be normal again? What was next? Just when I thought things were getting better, we went two steps back. John was quiet all that Sunday afternoon.

Of course, Mrs. Jenkins could see the worry in my eyes as soon as I stepped on her porch the next day. "Chile, what's wrong with you now? You look as anxious as a one-eyed cat watchin' two rat holes."

Even Mrs. Jenkins couldn't bring a smile to my face that day. "We've got a problem, Mrs. Jenkins; Shelly's gone certifiable. She thinks John still cares for her, and she won't stop calling him. She even took the boys out to lunch last Sunday and tried to act like their mother."

"Bless!" Mrs. Jenkins gasped. "What woodpile did she crawl out of? Whatcha gonna do now?"

"I haven't a clue. I'm worried about John. I've never seen him so mad." I started chewing my nails nervously.

"Who wouldn't be mad? Sounds like he's got hisself in a tight spot." Mrs. Jenkins shook her head. "Ya know, my Bert whooped the tar outta one of my admirers oncet. Maybe you should brush up on yer whoopin' skills."

"I'm afraid I would get the short end of the stick, Mrs. Jenkins. She'd probably end up 'whoopin' me."

"Yeah, you ain't big as a fart knocker."

Standing up, I said, "I guess we'll just have to take one day at a time. Maybe she'll soon realize that it's pointless and leave us alone."

"I hope so, Josie. Don't go lettin' that piece a' trash ruin yer life."

"Thanks for everything, Mrs. Jenkins. You need any stamps today?"

"Nah. I'm good. Don't you worry none. Things will all work out, just you watch."

That evening, I was in the kitchen fixing dinner when John came stomping in, throwing things around and growling like a bear.

I wiped my hands on a kitchen towel and asked, "What in the world is wrong with you?"

"Shelly! That's what's wrong!" I stood there with dread, wondering what she had done this time. "I had to go by the office and drop off some paperwork, and she was there waiting in the parking lot. She stood in my way trying to stop me, saying all kinds of crap and causing a scene. I swear, I don't know how much more I can take, Josie." Sitting down on the couch he hung his head in frustration.

"John, we need to go to the police. This has gone on long enough."

"I don't know. It's so humiliating."

"Tomorrow, we're going to go and get it over with. This is ridiculous! I'm not going to let her ruin our lives and involve our children."

John nodded, knowing there was no other way.

I called the police department that night and found out that we would have to pick up a restraining order packet at the courthouse, then wait for a judge or magistrate to become available. If it was serious enough, they would grant the order immediately. I prayed that they would.

I took a day off from work and John and I went first thing the next morning so we could put it behind us. After waiting for what seemed like ages, the judge deemed the order be considered immediate, and directed us to the sheriff's department so they could serve the papers to Shelly. I felt good because we had at least accomplished something. After taking me home, John went back to work, trying to make up for lost time.

I had a lot of time that afternoon to sit and think about everything that had happened. I knew that Shelly had always had a little crush on John, but I never dreamed of how bad it really was. Had all her failed relationships been because of her obsession with John, instead of them not living up to her high expectations, as she had claimed? All these years she had pretended to be my best friend, but was secretly lusting after my husband! It was amazing, really, and I felt so stupid for not seeing the signs.

After John told me the truth, memories would pop up out of nowhere of things that had happened in the past. One time I had invited Shelly and Jared over for dinner and cards, and Shelly had been flirting with John. I didn't think too much of it at the time, because she always flirted with whatever guys were around; John was no exception. This time in particular, though, she and Jared had left early because they had been arguing. John had been awfully quiet that night too. Had something happened between Shelly and John, and once again I had been oblivious?

Feeling a headache coming on from all the stress, I took some medicine and got back in bed, turning all the lights off.

I woke up with John lying beside me. I pulled him towards me and held him tight. His body was trembling and I told him, "It's going to be okay, John. I love you so much. We'll get through this, I promise."

A few days later, I was served with a restraining order to stay away from Shelly. Because I had made a scene at her place of work and because several witnesses were available, I was deemed a threat. Could this get any worse? Unbelievably it could, and would.

Chapter 30

John was livid when he found out I had been served. If Shelly had been standing near him, she would have breathed her last breath. Once again, I tried to calm him down, even though I was mad and frustrated too. Things like this happened to other people, not us. The news covered situations like this all the time, and I would just shake my head, marveling at how crazy people were but never imagining I would be caught up in my own drama. As much as I was upset, I worried more about John. He blamed himself for everything.

I continued to visit my father, and he continued to decline daily. Mary and I didn't talk anymore about her plans after Dad died. If we were in dad's room at the same time, we sat mostly in silence, lost in our own thoughts. I usually thought about all the drama going on in my life; whatever Mary thought about was a mystery, one I wasn't privy to and probably never would be.

Spending time with David lifted my spirits like nothing else. I didn't want to burden him with all my problems, so I kept them to myself. I noticed right away that my painting was hanging in the living room, causing a special joy in my heart. The first time I saw my grandmother's artwork, I cried. I was so emotional; I didn't have the words to tell David how much it meant to me that he shared her work with me. Her artwork was beautiful, and incredibly professional. She had been so talented, and I would have given anything to be able to meet her. One day, David told me to pick out something for myself. I knew right away what I wanted: a landscape painting with wild flowers and mountains in the distance. The colors were soft, and I knew it would look perfect in the cabin. I couldn't wait to get it home and hang it up.

Driving home, I felt better than I had since I had been served with the restraining order. We hadn't heard anything from Shelly for about two weeks, and we were beginning to believe that it was finally over. It was almost 7:30 when I got home, and I saw the light on in the barn. I had picked up some fast food fried chicken, which I seemed to be doing a lot lately. It was easier, and by the time I got home I was usually tired and didn't feel like cooking.

John came in not long after I did, and actually looked relaxed for once. It made my heart leap, seeing him smile again. After we ate, we sat on the couch and watched television. *Andy Griffith* re-runs were on. It was an episode we'd seen a hundred times, but we smiled and laughed like it was the first time. It was such a mundane thing to do on a weeknight but after all that we had been through, we were very content.

John had his arm around me and I could feel his lips on my head. I wanted to hold onto the moment and not let go. Shelly could try all she wanted, but she would never come between John and I again. Our love had only grown stronger with everything life had thrown at us. I knew she would eventually give up. I'd had my back turned once, but never again.

John was chuckling at something Barney said to Andy when we heard knocking on our screen door.

We usually left the front door open in the evenings to let the cool breeze drift through the house. A man's voice said, "Anybody home?"

I looked at John with my eyes wide. Under my breath I said, "Who could that be?" We didn't get many visitors, especially on our little back country road.

John turned the television off and said, "Just a minute." We both got up and walked to the door.

A man in uniform was standing on the front porch with a grim look on his face. "Hey. I'm Officer Waldrop with the county police. You got a minute?"

John opened the door and said, "Sure, come on in." He walked in and I motioned for him to sit down on one of the chairs in the den. John and I sat down on the couch.

After confirming our names, he said, "I'm afraid I've got some bad news. Shelly Gibson was found dead in her house today. She was murdered." He stopped talking, making a mental note of our reactions.

My hand went straight to my mouth and I looked at John. He had such a look of panic in his eyes that I automatically took his hand, holding on for dear life. Would this nightmare ever end?

"Our records indicate that she had a restraining order against you, Mrs. Carrier. I'm sorry, ma'am, but I have to ask you your whereabouts today. Can you begin with the time you got up this morning?"

I started shaking uncontrollably. John said, "Look, she had nothing to do with this. Shelly was crazy and got the restraining order just because we put one on her first."

"Whatever the reason, I'm still obligated to fill out my report. Mrs. Carrier?"

I was in shock. I whispered, "Shelly's dead?" The officer nodded his head and waited for me to continue. "Oh my God. I can't believe this." I looked in desperation at John. He squeezed my hand and nodded. Encouraged, I said, "I...um...I went to work at seven thirty, and after finishing my postal route I clocked out about four o'clock. I changed out of my postal uniform, and...I'm sorry." Taking a deep breath and trying not to cry, I continued, "Then I went to see my dad at hospice. I stayed about an hour and then went to see my father." The officer looked confused so I said, "My real father. My dad who's in hospice raised me. Anyway, I stayed there until about six forty-five, went to the Chicken Hut to pick up dinner, and then came home. I got here close to seven thirty."

"On your route, do you drive your own car or a postal vehicle?"

"Postal vehicle."

"I'll need the name and number of your supervisor. I'll also need your dad's and the hospice phone number so I can verify that you were there, as well as your real father's name and number. Do you happen to have a receipt for your dinner?"

"Yes. Hold on, I'll get it." I jumped up from the couch and ran into the kitchen. I was rummaging through the trash, trying to find the receipt. It was stapled to the bag, so I tore it off and brought it back and gave it to the officer.

After giving him the rest of the information, the officer said, "Mr. Carrier, I'll need your whereabouts, as well."

John said, "When was she murdered?"

"I'm not at liberty to say, Mr. Carrier. What time did you leave for work this morning?"

Sighing deeply, John said, "I left about seven o'clock this morning. I went by the office, then left for a job soon after in Kingsport. I worked there until about eleven, finished up, and ate my lunch in my truck. I went to another job in Bristol around twelve-thirty. I worked there until about five-thirty, then dropped my paperwork off at the office and came straight home."

"What did you do once you were home?"

"I've been working in the barn. I have a tractor that's broken down, and I'm trying to get it running again."

"Okay, I'll need the name and number of your place of employment."

Once John and I gave the officer all the information he had requested, he thanked us both for our time and then left. I immediately let the tears fall down my face and cried in John's arms. We stood that way for a while and then I said, "Shelly's dead! I can't believe it! Who would murder her, John?"

"I certainly wanted to, but someone beat me to it."

"John! Please don't say that. Don't even joke about it."

"Josie, I won't apologize. She made my life a living hell. She deserved everything she got."

I looked at John as if he was a stranger. How could he say things like that? Yes, she made a lot of mistakes...but murder? "Oh my word! I've got to call David and tell him what's going on before they call him. What will he think of me? I'm a murder suspect, for goodness' sake. He definitely won't want anything to do with me now."

"Josie, don't say that."

"Well, it's true!" I walked over to the phone and started dialing before I lost my nerve. When he answered, I said, "David, I have something terrible to tell you. I'm so sorry but..." I started crying and couldn't stop. John took the cordless phone from me and then went into the other room. I walked over to the window and looked outside, staring at nothing. How would we get through this hurdle? John and I were both innocent, so who killed Shelly? Had she pushed some other person until they pushed back, snuffing the light right out of her? Was she shot, stabbed, or choked to death? Poor Carly! What was she going to do?

John came up behind me and pulled me against him. "Your father wanted me to tell you that he loves you more than ever, and that he's here for both of us whenever we need him." I closed my eyes in relief, but still felt ashamed. I didn't want to drag his name into this mess; he didn't deserve it. "I'm sorry about what I said earlier, Josie. Shelly was a bad person, but she didn't deserve to be killed."

We went to bed that night with heavy hearts. The coming days would probably test us like nothing else. We clung to each other, trying to draw enough strength to help us survive this nightmare we found ourselves in. I prayed the police would find the real killer and leave us alone. I thought about the lesson in church last week, to "stay strong in the Lord" and to "stand firm." Shelly was dead. Someone had actually murdered her. I looked up and thought, *I'm trying God!*

Chapter 31

Matthew called me on my cell phone the next day while I was delivering mail. He sounded worried and on edge. "I just heard about Carly's mom. What's going on?"

"Oh, honey, it's a long story. Can you and Tyler come over? We need to talk."

"Yeah; I'm off tonight and Tyler gets off about six, so we'll come over as soon as we can."

I stopped at Mrs. Jenkins house. I knew she would be crazy with questions, because Shelly's murder was all over the news.

She didn't say anything as I walked on the porch. She just grabbed me and pulled me into a tight hug. Her slight frame squeezed harder than I thought possible. Patting me on the back, she said, "You poor thing. I've thought and thought about ye."

Wiping my tears, I said, "I don't know how much more I can take, Mrs. Jenkins."

We both sat down, lost in our own thoughts. Bert came out with some iced tea and patted me on the hand. I whispered, "Thank you, Bert," before he walked back inside.

Mrs. Jenkins said, "I'm prayin' that they find the real killer quick like, so it'll be over. Just hang in there chile; it'll all work itself out."

"Thank you, Mrs. Jenkins. I hope you're right."

John called me from work while I was on my route to check on me. I told him to come home as soon as he could because the boys were coming over. I heard him sigh and then say that he would be there as soon as he could. After I got home, I decided to take some ibuprofen and lay down before my headache got any worse. Eventually, John walked in looking like he had walked to hell and back. I knew he dreaded telling the boys, and didn't want to see the disappointment in their eyes. They had always worshiped the ground John walked on but would soon find out that he wasn't infallible, and only human after all.

Matthew and Tyler both had somber faces as they walked in the door. Tyler hugged me and said, "I can't believe that Carly's mom is dead. Who would have done such a thing?" Matthew looked troubled, so I knew he must have known about the restraining orders and that we were questioned.

John said, "Boys, sit down, I need to tell you something." After clearing his throat, John said, "I didn't want you to find out this way—actually, I didn't want you to find out at all—but I made a terrible mistake. I...I stepped out on your mom, with Shelly. Because of some things that have happened, we're being questioned regarding her murder. We're innocent, of course, but until they find the person who did this, our lives will be upside down."

The boys sat staring at us in stunned silence, disbelief on their faces.

Matthew jumped up and yelled, "How could you cheat on mom like that?! And with her, of all people?"

"I know. It's unforgivable, but your mom has taken me back. I'm sorry, boys. I wish I could turn back time. You don't know how bad I wish that, but I can't."

I finally found my voice and said, "We both have blame in this. You know I was in a deep depression after mamaw died."

"But that doesn't give Dad the right to do that!"

"No, boys, it doesn't. But it's more complicated than that. We can't explain everything we've both been through, so you'll just have to try and understand. Don't judge, just know that we're okay now, that I love your father and he loves me."

I looked at John and his eyes were closed, pain evident in his expression. "Your father and I have worked everything out and are closer than ever. All we can do now is pray that they find the person who murdered Shelly, and that he or she pays for what they've done. No matter what she did, she didn't deserve this."

Tyler never said a word. He just sat there in shock.

Matthew sat back down and shook his head. "I can tell you that it doesn't look good. You need to find a lawyer, because they're going to look for someone with motive. From what you say, it sounds like you both have motive."

In frustration, I said, "But we didn't do anything, and we have nothing to hide. We could never hurt Shelly. Yes, we were mad, and yes, we wanted her out of our lives, but we didn't kill her!"

"You still have to protect yourselves."

Matthew knew what he was talking about. The next evening, a police officer came to the house and took John in for questioning. I panicked; not knowing what to do, I called David. "Slow down honey, tell me one more time."

"They just came by the house and took John back to the police station for more questioning. What do I do, David?" I started crying again, unable to control my emotions.

"I'm going to call my lawyer, Austin Harris; he's a close family friend. He'll stop the police from any unnecessary interrogation. Don't worry, he'll be home soon." I breathed a sigh of relief and thanked him for helping us.

David's lawyer brought John home, and we went over all the details of the case. He told us that he would do his best to represent us and for us to try not to worry. They didn't have any evidence against John other than possible motive, and even that was weak. All they needed to do was find someone that had more motive than us.

After he left, John and I walked into the house and sat down on the couch. I crossed my arms, waiting for John to tell me what happened at the police station. He told me that because there was nobody at the jobsite the day Shelly was murdered, they couldn't verify that he was there the whole time, even though he finished all of the electrical work.

I couldn't understand why this would be a problem. "Couldn't someone say that the work you did took X amount of hours?"

John just shook his head and said, "Apparently that's not good enough."

On the news, they indicated that Shelly had been bludgeoned to death. John said, "They kept asking me if I had any hammers. Can you believe that? I said I own a farm! Of course, I had hammers, multiple hammers! I've got a few other tools that could have done the job too." In a fit of anger, John stood up and threw his truck keys across the room, hitting a clock on the wall. It fell with a loud crash.

My hand went to my chest in alarm. "You didn't tell them that did you?"

"No. I'm not that stupid." John turned and looked at me with frustration filling his eyes. "What scares me, though, is that if she wasn't dead, I believe I could kill her with my bare hands." With that shocking statement, John walked to the bedroom and slammed the door. I fell on my knees and prayed as hard as I could pray, then I called our pastor. I felt so much comfort just knowing he was praying for us. He said he would call a meeting of our church deacons and they would pray for us too.

John came home early the next day. The company he worked for had asked him to take a paid leave of absence until the matter was resolved. They believed in his innocence, but felt it was best if he took some time off. John had worked there for more than 20 years, and they trusted him, but he felt as if he had let them down. He looked miserable and depressed, and I didn't know what to do to help him.

I found him out in the barn later that evening. He was putting some tools up. John always kept the barn neat and orderly—not like my father, who had left things lying around everywhere. I couldn't help but think of the last time I had been in the barn and heard him talking to Shelly. My world had turned upside down, and I thought our marriage was over. It felt like ages ago.

Ricky jumped up when he saw me and began rubbing against my legs. John look startled and turned quickly, wiping his face, but not before I saw the tears glistening in his eyes. My heart went out to him. I waited a few seconds, then walked up behind him silently. As I put my arms around him, I felt him suck in his breath, trying to hold back tears. I held him until I felt him let go; great big sobs poured from his being. He turned around and we held each other, both crying.

"John, just let it out. I promise as long as we have each other everything will be okay." John nodded, squeezing me tighter. "I love you so much, and I'll always be by your side."

Taking his handkerchief out of his pocket, John blew his nose. "I couldn't make it without you, Josie. I just feel like I've let everyone down. Seeing the boys faces when I told them just about killed me. And what I said about Shelly...I didn't mean it."

"I know you didn't, John. I know that with all my heart. Just take a few deep breaths, and then let's go through a drive-thru somewhere and get some ice cream. My treat." I smiled and put my arms around his neck, standing on my toes. "I could really go for a banana split."

"Then you shall have your banana split. Anything for you." John kissed me softly. "Thanks for being you."

"Think about that later when I'm a couple pounds heavier tomorrow." I winked and turned to leave. "Meet you at the truck!"

Chapter 32

Mary called the next morning and said, "I know you're going through a lot right now, but you need to come and see Dad. I don't think it's going to be much longer."

I hadn't even talked to Mary regarding Shelly's death. I figured she knew about it, since it was plastered all over the local news. But once again, she didn't presume it was any of her business. It would have been nice if my sister had called to check on me to make sure I was okay.

John and I went that night, and I was shocked to see the difference in Dad. The nurses told us that all of his organs were shutting down, and it wouldn't be long. He was on some heavy pain medication, but no longer on any kind of fluids. I prayed that God would take him quickly, because he had already suffered enough. I got the call in the middle of that night that he had passed and I could only feel relief. I loved him, even though I never felt much love in return. I tried not to blame him. Who knows what he went through, when he found out about Mom's affair and resulting pregnancy? He fed me, clothed me, and made sure I had everything I needed. I would always be thankful for that.

I thought back to when I was learning how to drive. Dad took me out in the old farm truck and we went up down those back country roads until I finally felt comfortable enough to take my driver's license test. He never hugged me, but he did pat me on the back and told me I did a good job. It wasn't much, but it was the best he could do. And somehow, I realized that.

Mary and I went together to make funeral arrangements. We decided on a simple gray casket, because Dad never was one for show. Mary made most of the decisions, but I wanted to be there for moral support. The funeral home had a nice chapel that we would use for the funeral. There would be a private burial immediately following the service.

We were in the funeral director's office, waiting to talk to the director to clear up some last-minute details. I looked at Mary, wondering what she would do now. Would she quit her job and start over somewhere else?

"Mary, I'm sorry I got mad when I told you about Dad."

She shook her head. "I shouldn't have been so glib about it, either. I'm sorry I said what I did."

"You mean about chasing butterflies and rainbows?" I smiled to let her know there were no hard feelings about that, either.

"Yes." Mary smiled one of her rare smiles.

"I guess we are pretty different."

Mary nodded. "I've heard all the news about Shelly. I'm sorry for everything you're going through, but I'm glad you and John got back together. I know he messed up, but I also know he loves you."

I had to shake myself because real conversations with Mary were very unusual. "I appreciate it. We're getting through it. I love John too, and we'll be fine. I just hope they catch the person who killed Shelly."

Our conversation ended when the director returned to his office, but the camaraderie was still there and it felt nice. Maybe there was hope for us yet. I knew our mom in heaven would be happy to see us getting along.

The funeral was fitting, and more people than I expected showed up. It's funny, how people you never met or didn't remember having met show up and talk about your dad like he was one of the nicest fellas around. Family members I hadn't seen in years came and paid their respects to Mary and I. It was nice, but exhausting. I could tell Mary was as tired as I was, probably more so. Aunt Betty, Dad's sister, felt that it was her responsibility to hang around until the end. Once she left, John and I sat down in one of the Victorian sofas scattered around the room.

Mary sat down in the chair next to it with a sigh. "Good grief, that was trying. If I had to do this again anytime soon, I think I'd kill myself first."

John smiled while I slipped my shoes off and put my legs on the sofa. "Can you believe so many people came? I figured there would be a handful at most. Did you see Cousin Janie? My goodness, that girl has put on a few pounds."

"A few?" Mary blew her cheeks out. "More like a hundred!"

I giggled. "And did you meet cousin Allen? No, Alvin, I think. He sure was a talker. He's in the insurance business in Marion."

Mary rolled her eyes. "Yes. I heard *all* about it. He cornered me for at least thirty minutes! When he pulled out his grandchildren's pictures, I feigned a headache and said I needed to go to the restroom." Mary pushed herself up and stood. "I'm sapped. Think I'll head on home."

John and I stood up as well. "Yeah. Us too. You need anything?"

Mary shook her head. "No. I'm just going to go home and sleep for a week. I took a few days off."

I nodded and we all walked outside. I wanted to hug Mary, but I held myself back. John and I turned towards the truck but before I could get in, Mary was there and put her arms out. I walked into them and held her tight. We both cried for a few seconds, and then she was gone.

Once we got home, I headed straight for the porch and sat in the rocker. John joined me, and we rocked companionably without talking for a while. With everything that was going on with Shelly's death, I had really needed the closeness I'd shared with Mary earlier. I felt John take my hand.

"What are you thinking about?"

I sighed. "I was just thinking how nice it was to talk to Mary. Do you know how long I've waited to have a real sisterly relationship with her?"

John just smiled. "I know we'll never be best friends, but it's nice to be able to just talk. You know?"

"Yeah. I know it means a lot to you."

"I know nothing about her personal life. It's weird." I shook my head. "Maybe she'll let me in one day." I looked at John. "I do know one thing. I'm so tired. I don't remember that last time I had a good night's sleep. I know you're the same."

John did look incredibly weary. "I'm okay."

"John, you're not okay. You're stressed, and plum pooped." I got out of my chair and climbed up in his lap. I kissed his forehead. "Poor man." I took his face in my hands. "I wish I could make it all better. Maybe once this is all over, we can go on vacation...a cruise, maybe. Wouldn't that be nice?"

John's arms wrapped around my middle. "That would be amazing, but I would just take normal."

"I agree." We sat rocking gently. The sound of a frog croaking nearby was typical of the noise we would hear at night on the farm, but it sounded so comforting and ordinary on that night. I remember in science class Mr. Ford told us it was only the male frogs that croaked. Sometimes the sounds would be more like barks or whistles. If you listened closely and let yourself be in the moment, you would be rewarded with a charming serenade.

The phone rang and interrupted our moment. With dread, I walked into the house. I didn't think I could stand more bad news. Answering the phone on the third ring, I said, "Hello."

"Hello, Mrs. Carrier? This is Austin Harris. I've got some great news for you. They've had a break in the case. Can I talk to John?"

With my heart racing, I rushed to the porch and handed the cordless phone to John. "It's Austin Harris. It's good news this time! They've had a break in the case."

John took the phone and stood up. I didn't hear much of the conversation and was on pins and needles when he finally hung up.

"Well? What did he say?" I was about to burst with anticipation.

John sat there shaking his head in disbelief. Finally, he rubbed his forehead and said, "Apparently Shelly's ex-husband, Jared, doesn't have an alibi. And he's definitely got motive."

Confused, I said, "What do you mean?"

"In their divorce agreement, Shelly was allowed to keep the house until Carly left for college, which of course was a couple of years ago, but then she was supposed to sell it. She'd been doing everything she could to delay it, and even threatened to sue Jared, saying that he had more money than he claimed on his taxes. She called the IRS and turned him in for tax fraud. They're thinking she pushed him a little too far."

Even though Shelly had badmouthed Jared to John and I numerous times, he had always been nice to us. Could he actually kill Shelly? Did he fly into a rage and beat her to death? I didn't want to think that was possible, but whoever it was had some kind of grudge against her.

I thought of poor Carly and what she must be going through. What would she do if she found out her father killed her mother? I couldn't imagine the devastation she must be going through. I stepped into John's arms and we held each other tight, both of us conflicted. We were glad that the focus was no longer strictly on John, but we were worried about Carly.

Chapter 33

The first thing John did the next day was call the office and tell them the situation. They agreed that under the circumstances, he could come back. They were short-handed anyway, and missed John immensely. I wondered why he couldn't just enjoy the time off, but John needed to keep busy; it wasn't in his blood to lie around and do nothing.

My parents' lawyer's office called and wanted Mary and I to come in for the reading of the will. It was a dreary day, and the rain couldn't decide if it wanted to make an appearance or not. Grabbing my umbrella, I walked out the door ready to get the day over with. Once we were seated across from Mr. Stewart at his desk, Mary and I sat there stiffly, waiting to hear what our future held. Would Mary get mad if it wasn't what she expected? Would I?

After the reading, Mary and I were both stunned into silence. With all the confusing technical terms, I asked the lawyer to please repeat it, but to put it in terms that I could understand.

"Basically, Mary will receive the farm house and five acres. Josie, you will receive the barn, all other out buildings, and four hundred and ninety-five acres. The insurance policy of one hundred thousand dollars will be divided equally between the both of you, as well as what's left in your parents' checking and savings accounts." He asked if we had any further questions. Seeing we had none, he said, "I have something for both of you that your mother wanted me to give you upon your father's death." He gave us both a sealed envelope with our names on it.

I looked at Mary and she had an unreadable expression on her face. With an appalled look on her face, she got up and said, "Well, I should have known I would be left with a hundred-year-old house that's about to fall in the ground. Mom made sure you got what you wanted, though." Bending down to pick up her pocketbook, she placed the envelope in the side pocket. Mary then turned and left the lawyer's office.

I closed my eyes and realized our earlier truce had come to an end. I was happy that we didn't have to break up the farm, but sad that once again Mary and I were distanced. Mr. Jackson cleared his throat, reminding me that I wasn't alone. Being an estate lawyer, I'm sure he ran into this sort of conflict all the time.

"Thank you, Mr. Stewart." I stood up and put my hand out.

Taking my hand and shaking it, he said, "Try not to worry, Josie. Your mom did what she thought was best. She worried about you girls."

I smiled and nodded. "Yes." I looked down at the envelope in my hand and wondered what words were inside. Closing my eyes, I held it against my chest, thankful I had something that came straight from my mom's heart. At that moment, I missed her more than ever. I needed her love and her words of encouragement, but I needed her comforting arms most of all.

I left the office and headed to my car. Once there, I realized I had left my umbrella and headed back. Something caught my eye in the corner of the parking lot and I noticed Mary's car. Mary and a man I didn't recognize were standing next to the driver's side door. They were talking, and the man put his hand on Mary's shoulder. Shaking my head, I got my umbrella and left for home.

I put some chicken and vegetables in the Crockpot and then took my letter and went to the front porch. I had a feeling that whatever was in the letter was very important so with eager anticipation, I began reading.

My dear sweet Josie,

I guess since you're reading this letter, your father has departed this world. I pray that he didn't suffer, and that he wasn't too much of a burden on you girls. I also hope that Mary understands the reasoning behind the will. I knew in my heart that she didn't want the farm, and would want to sell her half. I also knew that it would put a great burden on you and John if she did. My hope is that you will keep it, and hopefully one day the boys will enjoy it as much as we did. I want you to know how very much I love you and I would never want to hurt you, but Josie, I have something to tell you that will change your life. I wish I'd had the courage to tell you years ago, but I just couldn't. I didn't want you to think less of me, or look at your father differently. When I married Paul, I wasn't really in love with him. I was young and couldn't wait to get out of the house. My father was physically and emotionally abusive, and my mother was a weak woman who had been brainwashed into believing everything was her fault. We all lived in fear of the day he would lose it completely. Then Paul came into my life, and I thought that he would be the answer to all of my problems. We married quickly. I knew right away it was a mistake, but I had no other choice but to lie in the bed I had made for myself. I eventually became restless, and I let my guard down in the worst way. I met the most wonderful man, and he made me feel alive and beautiful. David was everything Paul wasn't. He was sweet, thoughtful, and he adored me. He looked at me the way your John looks at you. I knew it was wrong, and I tried so hard to stay away from him—but in the end, I gave in and I became pregnant with you. I told your father everything; he begged me not to leave him, and promised me that he would raise you as his own. Although I wanted to leave him, I felt guilty and ashamed of what I had done. In the end, I couldn't leave even though I loved David. I know your dad didn't always treat you and Mary equally, and I'm sorry, but I know he did the best he could. I hurt two people with my actions because I broke David's heart and let your dad down. David wanted to marry me and was ready to leave everything for me, but I begged him to let me go. His last name is Murray. The last I heard, he still lived in town and wasn't married. I'm sorry for all the pain and hurt that I've caused, but having you was all worth it. I love you, Josie, and I can't wait to see you in heaven.

Love,

Mama

I was crying uncontrollably by the time I finished the letter. I cried for all the heartache she'd endured in her life, and for what could have been. I cried for her, for David, and for myself, and thought about how sad life could be. I also thought how lucky I was to be married to the love of my life. Even though we've gone through something that would tear most marriages apart, we came back stronger than ever.

I knew I had to call David and tell him about the letter. "She loved you, David, but she just couldn't leave Dad."

"Your mama was a wonderful woman. I miss her every day."

"It breaks my heart that she lived such a sad life."

"She had you, Josie. If you've made her half as happy as you've made me, then she was a lucky woman."

"You're never going to believe what was in the will. Mary is definitely not happy. She got the house and five acres, but the rest was left to me, all four hundred and ninety-five acres. She'll probably sell the house as soon as she can." I still couldn't believe it. Of course, she could always contest the will.

David said, "Who knows? Maybe I'll buy it if she would sell it to me."

"Really? That would be awesome! I would give anything to have you live there." I had no idea what his financial situation was, but if he bought that house, he would have to sink a lot of money in it.

I was stirring my chicken and vegetables when John got home. He walked behind me, moving my hair away from my neck to nuzzle it, causing me to shiver. "You keep that up, buddy, and you won't get much work done this evening." I turned around and put my arms around his neck.

John pushed me against the counter. "No, but I'll have more fun." After giving me a few kisses that made my head spin, he whispered, "How'd it go today?"

"It was interesting, I can tell you that." I told John about the will, the letter, and then about what I saw in the parking lot. "She never talks about anything personal. I wonder who he was..."

John shrugged and walked to the refrigerator, getting a bottle of water. "It sounds like she's got a fella."

My brow wrinkled. "Maybe, but he seemed awfully young for her."

John smiled and took a drink of water. "Maybe that's why she hasn't introduced us, and why she's so secretive."

I shook my head. "I thought she had given up on men." I didn't know what to think about this new revelation. I wish Mary felt like she could talk to me. Did she think I would judge her harshly? After what happened in the lawyer's office, I figured that if we'd ever had a chance before, we wouldn't now.

Chapter 34

It was the end of August before they finally made an arrest in Shelly's murder. John and I watched the news together and saw Jared being taken into police custody in handcuffs. I couldn't help but feel some relief that it would finally be put behind us. I prayed for Carly, hoping that she would be able to persevere and hold her head high. I wanted to call her, but held myself back. Carly always seemed to have a lot more sense than her mother, so hopefully she would be all right.

It was time for the boys to meet David, so I decided to invite everyone over for a Labor Day cookout. They still didn't know anything about him, so I was a little nervous. I invited Mary as well, but figured I was wasting my time. I left a rambling message on her voicemail. I was sure it sounded crazy and I cringed, thinking about her listening to it. I'd even said, "I'll try to keep all the unicorns away."

I stopped by Mrs. Jenkins' house and invited her and Bert over, too. "I would love for you to meet David, Mrs. Jenkins. He would think you're a real hoot."

"I jes' bet he would. I guess me 'n Bert better stay around here. His hoity-toity daughter's a-comin' for her oncet a year visit." She definitely didn't look too happy about it.

"Why does she come Labor Day instead of Thanksgiving or Christmas?"

"Heck if I know! Guessin' those holidays is too important for her old dad and step-mom." Whispering, she said, "Don't bother me none; I'd be happy if she never came 'round. I can't cuss or even let a little wind ruffle my dress without her a-fussin'."

Laughing, I said, "Well, you're welcome to bring them if you want. The more the merrier."

"I wouldn't want to ruin yer party. 'Sides, her man would eat ya out of house an' home." She shook her head and continued, "No, we better jes' stay here, especially if we go to fist city. We orta just lock up and take off for Dollywood. I heerd her royal highness herself was in this weekend. Bert's crazy 'bout Dolly; says I'm her spittin' image."

I smiled. "Okay. Let me know if you change your mind. I just hope the heat lets up. I'm ready for some cooler weather."

"Not me. My old joints are rustin' up, and they like it hot—the hotter the better."

Smiling, I stood up and stepped off the porch. "Gotta go now. Good luck with your company."

The morning of the cookout promised to be another warm day. David arrived first. The three of us sat on the front porch and waited on the boys. David said, "You know, I was serious about buying the house. What do you think about it? I wouldn't want to overstep my bounds."

I smiled and said, "I told you I would love it, and I really would. I think it would be awesome having you so close."

David looked at John and John said, "Sounds good to me, but I hope you know what you're getting into. The house has some good bones but it's old, and needs a lot of work. We'll help you all we can, though."

"That's not a problem. If you see Mary, let her know I'm interested." We sat there talking about the house and all the improvements that would be needed when the boys pulled up. Standing up, we all walked down the front porch steps, waiting on Matt and Tyler. They noticed David and both nodded to him in greeting.

"Boys, I have someone I want you to meet. This is David. David, this is Matthew and Tyler." They shook hands, and I took a deep breath before I explained. "I have something crazy to tell you; David is my father, and your grandfather." They looked confused so I added, "I just found out a few weeks ago myself."

Matthew blinked, unable to comprehend, and Tyler stood there with his mouth hanging open. David put his arm around me and said, "It's true; I've known for a long time, but I promised your grandmother I wouldn't contact your mother. When your mother found out and called me, it was one the happiest days of my life."

Laughing, Tyler exclaimed, "Dang, Mom! What else is going to happen around here? I used to think you guys were the most boring people on earth, but now... Well, now it's like a soap opera around here."

We all started laughing and I hugged them both. "We'll try and tone it down from now on. Glad that's out of the bag. Now, who's hungry? John, can you start the burgers?" I went back into the house, glad to have something to keep my hands and mind busy. By the time I got everything out and on the table, John began bringing the burgers in. I walked outside to tell David and the boys that dinner was ready, but stopped to watch them for a moment when I saw them talking and smiling as if they've known each other for a long time. David had that effect on people. He knew exactly what to say to make you feel comfortable. My heart soared, but at the same time I thought about how sad it was that we were just now able to have the relationship we should have had all along. Trying not to dwell on anything negative, I hollered, "Come and get it!"

We all ate until we were stuffed. I told everyone we would cut the watermelon later, when our food had settled a bit. Relaxing on the porch, we talked about everything, from sports to farming, and then the boys told us funny stories about work. Tyler had dealt with a guy dressed up like a woman, stealing perfume and jewelry at the department store. He stuffed necklaces and bracelets in his bra and nobody wanted to fish them out, least of all Tyler. Matthew told us about a bunch of burglaries that turned out to be some teenagers on drugs, and they were all from well-to-do families. One was the daughter of a prominent doctor. It was all over the local news.

David told us that he had owned and operated a local convenience store for several years. They had been robbed more times than he could count. He told a funny story about an old man who was so drunk one night that he called 9-1-1 on himself. After apologizing to everyone, he sat on the curb right outside the store and cried until the cops came and arrested him. We were talking and laughing so much that we didn't even notice when Mary walked up to the porch with the same man I'd seen at our lawyer's office.

I stood up and said, "Mary, I'm glad you could come. Let me fix you both a plate."

They walked about halfway up the steps. "We've already had dinner. Thanks anyway. This is my friend, Rick Palmer."

"Hi, Rick, I'm Josie. This is my husband John, my father David, and my two sons, Matt and Tyler. It's very nice to meet you."

Rick smiled and said, "It's nice to meet you, too."

Mary looked at me and said, "I just wanted you to know that I'm moving out of the farmhouse. I'm going to contact a realtor and put it on the market. I'll let you know if anyone is interested. Also, if there's anything personal there that you want, let me know."

"As a matter of fact, Mary, David is interested in buying the house." I turned to David and smiled.

Standing up, David said, "I would very much like to talk to you about the house, whenever it's convenient for you."

Mary looked a little surprised. "Okay. Well, I'll get your number from Josie and call you soon, then."

David stepped down and shook her hand. Mary said, "It's nice to meet you." She looked up at the boys. "Hey boys, hope you're doing well."

As they walked back down the steps, Rick waved. "It was nice to meet you all."

After they left, I immediately wondered where Mary was moving to and if it was with Rick, but I didn't say anything. I glanced at John and he gave me a knowing look.

After we cut into the watermelon, everyone stayed for a little longer and then left for home. John helped me clean up the rest of the dishes and put the leftovers away. I smiled to myself, thinking how nice it was for him to do little things like this. As I was wiping the countertops, John came up behind me, placing his arms around me and his chin on the top of my head. "Let's go for a walk. There's a full moon tonight, and not a cloud in the sky."

We used to go for walks all the time at the farm. Exploring was a favorite pastime for us. We often collected Native American arrowheads. John and the boys even found a Native American knife on the property. There were two caves, and even a small waterfall. John wasn't much of a hunter, but he did like to sit and watch for deer and other animals. We also had a bench out by the pond that John had built out of some of the fallen timber. We loved watching the ducks and listening to the frogs. Sometimes the deer would walk down from the mountains and drink water from the pond right in front of you, if you were real quiet.

Nodding I said, "Sounds great. Let me get a light sweater, just in case."

It was a little before dusk as we walked towards the pond, the dogs on our heels. I looked up at the farmhouse. Some of the lights were on and two cars were in the driveway. One was Mary's; the other must have been Rick's. My curiosity got the better of me and I said, "John, let's go over and say hi."

John just shook his head and said, "I don't think that's a good idea. Unless you have a valid excuse, you know she's just going to think you're a nosy britches, which you are."

"Aw, John; you're no fun! I can say I wanted to... Oh, I know, we can ask for Mama's big Crockpot. You know, the one that looks like it's big enough for a twenty-pound turkey? I'm sure Mary doesn't need it."

I could tell by the look on John's face that he wasn't buying it, and she probably wouldn't either. "First of all, leave me out of it. Second, that's lame and you know it. Let it go, Josie. Give Mary time, and let her do the socializing on her terms."

Curling my lip up in annoyance, I barked, "Fine!" I started walking faster to show that I was irritated. I wasn't paying very close attention and walked right into a spider web, and started jumping around and shrieking. I just *knew* baby spiders were crawling all over my body. I could hear John chuckling behind me, which irritated me even more. "You think that's funny? What if it was a bunch of black widow spiders and they bit me? You wouldn't be laughing if I died!"

"Don't you think you're being a little dramatic?"

"You know how I hate spiders! Next time a bat comes flying around and I hear you scream like a schoolgirl, I'm going to laugh at you! So there!" John had an unnatural fear of bats and detested them in every way.

"Okay, I'll stop laughing! Now come here, and let me make sure you don't have any spiders crawling on you." I tried to stand still, but my whole body was shaking with nerves.

John began to slowly examine me with his pocket flashlight and then stopped. His eyes began widening at an alarming rate and I shouted, "*What*?! What is it?!"

He couldn't help the smile that spread over his face. "Nothing; just kidding."

"*John Carrier!*"

Unfazed, John grabbed me and pulled me close and said, "Josie Carrier!" His lips stopped the next words out of my mouth. As his mouth covered mine, I quickly forgot what I was mad about. John stopped all of a sudden, taking my face in his hands. "Do you know how much I love you?"

In a daze, I whispered, "Not really. Why don't you tell me?"

"I love you more than I ever thought possible, and I can't believe you actually forgave me." John pulled me in his arms and held me tight. "I've got a surprise for you."

I stepped back and looked up. "Really? What is it?"

John took both my hands. "How would you like to go to the beach at the end of September? I know someone at work who will rent us their condo in Myrtle Beach for a week. We'll celebrate our anniversary just a little late."

"I wondered if you realized that we forgot it." I giggled. "Yes! I would love that."

"The condos are right on the beach. I've seen the pictures, and it looks real nice. The complex has its own swimming pool and restaurant."

"Sounds wonderful."

John took both my hands and brought them to his lips. "Good. It will be great. A whole week of being lazy, eating, sleeping, and..." John winked. "Well, we'll be in the bed a lot, but maybe not sleeping so much."

"Sort of like our honeymoon?"

John grinned. "Yeah...sort of like that."

Chapter 35

I told Mrs. Jenkins about the trip to the beach John had planned. "Well, I swany! The Carriers must be in high cotton!"

I laughed. "Not quite. Someone John works with has a small condo at Myrtle Beach. We're going to rent it for about a week."

"That in South Cackalacky?"

I laughed. "Yes. South Cackalacky."

"Well, I reckon you two need a little time away, but I'll miss ya. I sorta like it when you come and keep me company."

"How was your visit with Bert's daughter? Or should I ask?"

"Well... Bert's not too happy with me right now. Me and Miss High and Mighty got into a little squabble. Her and that good-fer-nothin' piece-of-you-know-what husband tried to get up all in my beeswax about us givin' them all we got when we kick the bucket. I told 'em they had some nerve. I could give my house and junk to anyone I wanted to, and it sure wouldn't be them!" Mrs. Jenkins had her arms crossed, and I could tell she thought Bert was eavesdropping. She kept glancing towards the door.

I didn't say anything because frankly, I wasn't sure what to say. Mrs. Jenkins continued, but she was talking more towards the kitchen door than to me. "This here house and property belong to me, and I can do whatever I want to with it. If they don't like it, they can kiss my flat butt!" I heard a deep "Harrumph!" from inside the house.

"Okay, I guess it didn't go so well. I hope you all can work it out, Mrs. Jenkins. Just remember, she *is* Bert's daughter; he loves her, flaws and all. Try not to let it bother you." I stood up because it was time to get back to work.

"I know." Lowering her voice to a whisper and talking out of the side of her mouth, she said, "She can't help she's ugly, but she could stay home." Mrs. Jenkins giggled at her own joke. I just shook my head and grinned as I waved goodbye.

Tyler called me later that afternoon while I was still delivering mail and asked if he could come by and talk to me about something. I was a little surprised; it wasn't like Tyler to come home to talk, especially by himself. That was the one thing I missed by not having a girl. I loved the closeness that my mom and I shared. Boys were different. They called me and texted me frequently, but not a lot about personal things.

Tyler was already sitting on the front porch when I pulled into our driveway. He was between Rick and Lucy, petting both dogs with a serious look on his face. Being the worrier that I am, I automatically assumed the worst. It had to be important for him to come all the way home to talk to me about it.

Looking at my sweet boy and wanting everything to be okay, I said, "What's up, Ty?" I used his nickname, the one that Matt gave him when he was little. He stood up and I pulled him into my arms, giving him a big squeeze.

"Mom, I have something I need to tell you." I sat down in the rocker, taking a deep breath to brace myself. After everything I had been through that summer, I knew that I would just have to stay strong. "Remember the last time you and Dad came over to our apartment, and I had been out late the night before?"

"Yeah, you had a 'hot date,' according to Matt." I smiled, trying to reassure him.

Tyler began rubbing the stubble on his chin and then said, "Well...I wasn't out with just anybody. I was with Carly." I couldn't help the look of shock on my face. He and Carly had always been good friends, but they never dated. Shelly and I had both encouraged them, but they were adamant about just being friends.

Looking at the mountains, Tyler said, "I don't know... Something happened. It was never right before, but all of a sudden it was different. Since then, with everything that's happened to her, we've grown even closer. I've wanted to tell you and Dad, but I didn't know how."

I closed my eyes and wished he was dating anybody but Carly. I had always loved Carly. She had stayed at our house so much when she was little, and she was like the daughter I never had. I just kept thinking of John and how he would feel. My gut told me that he wouldn't like it; every time she came around, it would remind him of Shelly. Things were finally getting back to normal, but this would set it all back again.

I had to ask Tyler the most important question I could think of. "Do you love her?"

"Yes. Mom, I'm crazy about her."

Releasing my breath, I said, "My goodness. I wasn't expecting this."

"I know. What do you think Dad will say?"

"I can't imagine he'll be happy about it, but it's not something he can't overcome. How does Carly feel? Will she be able to be around us, knowing what happened?"

"Actually, she blames her mother for most of it, and she wants nothing to do with her father now. I think she really misses you." I was so torn. I wanted to be there for Carly, but I knew John would have a hard time.

"Why don't you let me talk to your father, and I'll see if I can break it to him easy. So, this is serious? Are you sure this is what you want?" I could tell by Tyler's expression that it was definitely what he wanted.

Tyler nodded and said, "I've never felt this way before, Mom."

"Okay, then. Try not to worry. I'll take care of your father."

Tyler stood up and gave me a half-smile. I stood up too and he hugged me. "I love you, Mom."

"I love you, too, Ty." I took his face in my hands. "I've always loved Carly too. I'm glad you're happy. That's all we want."

After he left, I sat back down on the rocker and thought about what I would say to John. Maybe he would be fine and I was worrying for nothing. I had put some pinto beans in the Crockpot that morning and decided to fix some Mexican cornbread to go with it. Two of John's favorites meant at least he would be happy when he sat down at the table for dinner. I waited until he was almost finished before I gave him the news.

"You have got to be kidding me!" John was absolutely furious. "There is no way my son is dating Shelly's daughter! I won't have it." John got up from the table, threw his napkin down, and stomped into the bedroom.

Following on his heels, I said, "John, he's in love. You can't tell him he's forbidden to see Carly. He's twenty-one years old, for goodness sakes!"

As he furiously unbuttoned his work shirt, he said, "I don't care if he's forty-two! I'm his father, and I know what's best!"

I sat down on the bed, trying to be calm. Taking a deep breath through my nose and releasing it slowly, I tried another approach. "Look, John, Carly is not Shelly."

Standing there in his underwear, John looked at me with frustration. "No, but I'd never be able to look at Carly without thinking of her mother." He then pulled his jeans and t-shirt on and walked out of the house.

Falling back on the bed, I looked at the ceiling and murmured, "Well, that went well." The phone started ringing, breaking the silence of the house. Grabbing the phone on the nightstand, I said, "Hello?"

"How's my girl?" David's voice was so sweet. How did he know I need him at that moment?

"She's still here." I needed him but didn't want to burden him with one more Carrier family problem, so I kept my mouth shut with our new drama.

"Guess who just called me? Mary! She wants to discuss the house. I'm going over there tomorrow evening." He sounded excited, and it made my heart swell.

"That's wonderful! Do you need me to come with you?"

"I asked if you could come with me, but she wanted me to come alone." I could just hear her: "This is none of Josie's business."

"Of course she does. Don't worry, I'm fine. I'm definitely not surprised."

"Shouldn't she realize I'm going to tell you everything anyway?"

"That's just the way she is, David. I'm used to it."

"Well, it's not right. Anyway, I couldn't wait to tell you, and to thank you again for a wonderful dinner the other day. I can't tell you how happy I am. Being a part of your family has been a dream come true."

"You're no happier than this girl, let me tell you! I can't wait until you move into the farmhouse. Let me know what she says."

By the time John came back to the house it was already dark. I was already in the bed reading a book. John stood next to the dresser pulling off his t-shirt. After he tossed it in the hamper, he walked over and sat on the edge of the bed. He took off his watch and set it on the nightstand. I marked my book and closed it.

I finally broke the silence. "You okay?" John's shoulders slumped and his hand went to his forehead, rubbing it slowly. I rose up behind him and placed my hands on his shoulders, rubbing gently.

"I thought if I tried hard enough, I could pretend it never happened." John's hand found mine and squeezed.

I wrapped my arms around him. "Oh, John... Pretending is not going to make it go away. God and I already forgave you, but you have to forgive yourself too."

John started shaking, and a gut-wrenching sob tore through his whole body. "But I don't deserve forgiveness." John turned and said, "I don't know if I could forgive you if you did the same thing. How could I expect the same of you?"

Taking his face in my hands, I said, "John, I know you, and you would forgive me too. I have no doubts. The boys still love and adore their dad, except now they know you're not perfect. But nobody is! Tyler is so worried about what you'll think, but he really loves Carly, too. Please, try and accept this. It would mean the world to Tyler. It will be difficult at first, but I promise you it will get easier and easier with time."

John pulled me around until I was settled in his lap. We held each other for a few moments, then John kissed the top of my head. "I love you, Josie. What did I ever do to deserve you?"

I placed my hands on each side of John's face and looked into his beautiful green eyes. "I couldn't imagine being with anyone else, John." I kissed his forehead, each cheek, his nose, and finally his lips.

John fell back on the bed, pulling me with him. He rolled me until I was on my back and he was leaning down, his lips a few inches from mine. Words were not necessary. The love in his eyes told me all I needed to know, all that I would ever need to know.

Epilogue

I look back at that summer and still wonder how it could have been so difficult, yet bring John and I closer than ever. My whole life had turned upside down and shattered, but the pieces found their way back together and they fit better than before. I had my husband back and I had David, the kind of father I had always wished for. Even Mary and I grew closer. Through it all, I had my mother's love and God's help.

David bought and moved into the farmhouse by Christmas. He was able to turn it into something we were all proud of. The house was old, but there was nothing wrong that couldn't be fixed. The old wood floors were sanded down and polished, the walls painted, the kitchen updated, and a new heat pump installed. He didn't try to change it, but he did make it better. He left the artwork on the walls of the playroom because there would be grandchildren one day, and he wanted to have a place for them to play. He said he felt close to mama in that old house, and that made him happy.

When Carly first came to us it was awkward, but I took her in my arms and told her I was so sorry for everything she had been through, and let her know that we would always be there for her. Tyler and Carly got married as soon as they graduated from college. Matt lost his roommate, but he moved on; he said his new girlfriend Katie was a whole lot prettier and smelled better, too. They met while he was on a date with another girl. Katie was their waitress. Matt was so infatuated that he dropped his date off, then went straight back to the restaurant and asked her out. Of course, I got all of my information from Carly, who got it from Tyler. Matt didn't think it was anything his mother needed to know.

I loved Rick, Mary's new friend. Linda and Rick had met at the hospital while Rick's mother was being treated for a broken hip and Mary was her nurse. Mary moved into Rick's condominium in town after selling the farmhouse. Rick had been married once before, but never had children.

He was actually ten years younger than Mary, but was an old soul. He taught high school English. Rick told me in confidence that it was hard for Mary to be open about their relationship at first. She was embarrassed about being so much older. After getting to know Rick, I never even thought about the age difference.

Mary and I finally made steps in the right direction to building a better relationship. I loved my sister and wanted her to be a big part of my life. That Christmas, David invited us all over one Saturday for a small get together. Most of the repair work had been done, and it looked amazing. Mary couldn't believe how great the old house looked. It was a little ironic that David, the man mom had an affair with, was living there, but it worked. Life sure did have a funny way of working out. It would have been better if Mama was there but I knew she was there in spirit and watching out for us all.

I finally began painting again. I started my own business on the side and painted murals on children's bedroom walls, pediatric medical offices, church Sunday school rooms, and just about anywhere and everywhere there was a need. The boys helped me advertise on the internet; I even had my own web page. Our local newspaper did a story on my work, which generated even more business.

Mrs. Jenkins died a couple of years after my "summer of truth," as I dubbed it. She was feisty until the very end, but her poor heart was worn out. She refused to leave her house and go to the "horsepittle," as she called it; poor Bert had to wait on her hand and foot. I went to visit her almost every day to talk, and also to give Bert a break. I promised her I would look out for him, but he died not long after she did. His heart wasn't in the best shape either. Before he died, Bert and I would sit on the porch just like Mrs. Jenkins and I used to do. He told me the story of how they met at her first husband's funeral, at the funeral home where he was working. It was love at first sight. She asked him on a date before she left the funeral home, telling him that life was too short and she wasn't going to waste time. They were married within a month, much to the disappointment of his daughter. He told me that it wasn't always easy being married to a beautiful, spirited woman who always turned heads, but he knew that it was well worth it.

His daughter and son-in-law came in like vultures when he died, but left in a huff when they found out everything was left to the church. Their house wasn't worth much, but the Jenkins had kept a lot of money in their savings account. Preacher Godsey was jubilant, and declared that Mr. and Mrs. Jenkins were saints. I knew Mrs. Jenkins would get a big laugh out of that. The money turned out to be a real blessing. The church was old, and the Jenkins' bequest meant the repairs needed could be completed without the church going into a lot of debt.

I missed Shelly. I missed the closeness we once shared. I hated what she did, but I finally forgave her. Carley and I went to her grave one fall evening and I placed pink and purple flowers (her favorite colors) at her stone. We laughed at first because the pink and purple clashed with all the vibrant autumn colors, but then we both cried. We stood holding each other's hand and I promised Shelly that I would look after her daughter. I asked Carley for a few moments alone. Once she left, I got on my knees. I told Shelly that I forgave her for what she did, and that I still loved her. I would only remember the good times we shared, and cherish those wonderful years for the rest of my life

John and I learned an important lesson that summer: to never take our marriage for granted. As long as you put God first and then each other, everything else will fall into place. If you truly love each other, with His help you can overcome anything even when you think all hope is gone. Forgiveness isn't easy, but it's vital. Because He forgives us, we must forgive each other.

Acknowledgments

Special thanks to my family for their love and support, because without them I wouldn't have the confidence to proceed with my dreams. Thank you to my parents for buying a farm that inspired me in so many ways. Most especially, I thank God for his love and forgiveness, because without that I would be lost.

About the Author

Karen Bruce is married to Kenny Bruce and they live in rural Virginia. Their two grown sons are happily married with children of their own. You can contact Karen at www.karengbruce.com, Karen G. Bruce (Facebook/Instagram).

Coming Soon

Look for Karen's upcoming novel, *Jenna: A Heart Never Dies*. Jenna has just lost her husband to a drunk driver, but finds new love with the man who receives her husband's heart.

CPSIA information can be obtained
at www.ICGtesting.com
Printed in the USA
LVHW040857221121
704098LV00002B/141